MISTRESS OF HIS REVENGE

BY

CHANTELLE SHAW

First published in Great Britain 2016
By Mills & Boon, an imprint of HarperCollins*Publishers*
1 London Bridge Street, London, SE1 9GF

Large Print edition 2016

ISBN: 978-0-263-26187-5

Our policy is to use papers that are natural, renewable and recyclable products and made from wood grown in sustainable forests. The logging and manufacturing processes conform to the legal environmental regulations of the country of origin.

Printed and bound in Great Britain
by CPI Antony Rowe, Chippenham, Wiltshire

CHAPTER ONE

THE HONOURABLE HUGO FFAULKS—with two Fs—was drunk and being sick into a vase. Not just any vase, Sabrina noted, her lips tightening with annoyance. The vase was a fine example of early eighteenth-century English porcelain and had been valued at fifteen hundred pounds by an auction house that had recently catalogued the antiques at Eversleigh Hall.

Compared to the value of the hall's art collection, which included two Gainsboroughs and a portrait by Joshua Reynolds, fifteen hundred pounds was not a vast sum, but in Sabrina's current financial crisis she needed every penny she could lay her hands on and selling the vase would at least allow her to pay the staff's wages and the farrier's bill.

A frown crossed her smooth brow. If only horses did not need shoeing every six weeks.

The cost of the farrier, plus vet's bills, feed and hay meant that Monty was becoming an expense she simply could not justify. She had spoken to a reputable horse dealer who had assured her that she should get a good price for a seven-year-old thoroughbred, but the thought of selling Monty was unbearable.

She turned her attention to Hugo, who was now leaning on one of the other party guests and trying to stagger in the direction of the bar.

'Take him to the kitchen and get some black coffee into him,' Sabrina instructed Hugo's friend. She wished she could phone Brigadier Ffaulks and ask him to come and collect his son, but Hugo's parents had paid her a sizeable fee to organise a twenty-first birthday party at Eversleigh Hall. Hugo and fifty of his friends had arrived the previous evening and would be staying at the hall for the weekend. Tomorrow after breakfast—if any of them could face a full English breakfast—they would be able to enjoy clay-pigeon shooting on the estate and fishing in the private lake.

Opening up Eversleigh Hall for weddings and parties was the only way that Sabrina could afford the huge running costs of the estate until her father returned. *If he ever returned.* She quickly pushed her fears about the earl to the back of her mind with the rest of her worries and smiled at the elderly butler who was walking stiffly across the drawing room.

'I'd better fetch a mop and clear up the mess, Miss Sabrina.'

'I'll do it, John. I don't expect you to clear up after *my* guests.' She could not disguise the rueful note in her voice. The butler was well aware that she hated seeing Eversleigh Hall being treated carelessly by the likes of Hugo and his friends, who seemed to think that having money, and in some cases aristocratic titles, gave them the right to behave like animals. And that was an insult to animals, Sabrina thought when she caught sight of a female guest lighting up a cigarette.

'How many times must I repeat the "no smoking in the house" rule?' she muttered.

'I'll escort the young lady out to the garden,' John murmured. 'You have a visitor, Miss Sabrina. A Mr Delgado arrived a few minutes ago.'

She stiffened. 'Delgado—are you sure that was the name he gave?'

The butler looked affronted. 'Quite sure. I would hazard that he is a foreign gentleman. He said he wishes to discuss Earl Bancroft.'

'My father!' Sabrina's heart missed another beat. She took a deep breath and groped for her common sense. Just because the unexpected visitor's name was Delgado did not automatically mean that it was Cruz. In fact the likelihood was zero, she reassured herself. It was ten years since she had last seen him. The date their relationship had ended and the date a week earlier when she had suffered a miscarriage and lost their baby were ingrained on her memory. Every year, she found April a poignant month, with lambs in the fields and birds busy building nests, the countryside bursting with new life while she quietly mourned her child who had never lived in the world.

'I asked Mr Delgado to wait in the library.'

'Thank you, John.' Sabrina forced her mind away from painful memories. As she walked across the entrance hall, past the portraits of her illustrious ancestors, she tried to mentally compose herself. It was likely that the mystery visitor was a journalist sniffing around for information about Earl Bancroft. Or perhaps Delgado was one of her father's creditors—heaven knew there were enough of them. But in either case she was unable to help.

She had no idea where her father was, and since he had been officially declared a missing person his bank accounts had been frozen. Sabrina thought of the mounting pile of bills that arrived at Eversleigh Hall daily. Since the earl's disappearance she had used all of her savings to pay for the upkeep of the house, but if her father did not return soon there was a strong possibility that she would be forced to sell her family's ancestral home.

A week earlier in Brazil

'We have to face the facts, Cruz. Old Betsy is finished. She's given us the last of her diamonds and there's no point wasting any more of our time and money on her.'

Cruz Delgado fixed his olive-green eyes on his friend and business partner, Diego Cazorra. 'I'm convinced that Old Betsy hasn't revealed all her secrets,' he said with amusement in his voice. He could not remember now if it had been him or Diego who had christened the diamond mine they had bought as a joint venture six years ago Old Betsy, but the name had stuck.

'Your belief that there could be deposits of diamonds deeper underground is founded purely on speculation fuelled by rumour and the drunken ramblings of an old miner.' Diego lifted a hand to shield his eyes from the blazing Brazilian sun and glanced around the two-thousand-acre mine site.

The ochre-coloured earth was baked as hard as clay and lorry tyre marks criss-crossed the dusty ground. Directly above the mineshaft stood the tall metal structure of the head frame, looking like a bizarre piece of modern art, and next to it were the huge winding drums used to operate the hoist that transported men and machinery down into the mine. In the distance, the glint of silver denoted the river, and beyond it was the dense green rainforest. An alluvial processing plant stretched along one river bank, its purpose to recover diamonds found in sediment sifted from the river bed. But the best diamonds, those of gem quality and high carat weight, were hidden beneath the earth's surface and could only be retrieved by men and machinery tunnelling deep underground.

'I believe Jose's story of the existence of another mine, or at least an extension of the original mine,' Cruz said. 'It confirms what my father told me before he died, that Earl Bancroft had discovered some historic drawings of tunnels that run far deeper than we currently operate.'

Cruz removed his hat and swept his sweat-damp hair back from his brow. Like Diego, he was over six feet tall and his muscular physique was the result of years of hard physical labour working in the mining industry. Both men were deeply tanned, but Cruz's hair was black while

Diego's was dirty blond—evidence that his father had been a European, although that was all Diego knew about the man who had seduced his mother and abandoned her when she had fallen pregnant.

Cruz and Diego had been friends since they were boys growing up in a notorious *favela*—a slum in Belo Horizonte, the largest city in the state of Minas Gerais. When Cruz's father had moved his family north to the town of Montes Claros to find work in a diamond mine, Cruz had persuaded Diego to join them at a mine owned by an English earl. They had been excited by the idea of making their fortunes but it had been many years before they had struck lucky and too late for Cruz's father.

'The geological sampling and magnetotelluric surveys we commissioned showed up nothing of interest,' Diego pointed out. 'Do you really believe a story about an abandoned mine over modern scientific surveying techniques?'

'I believe what my father told me with his dying breath.' Cruz's jaw hardened. 'When Papai discovered the Estrela Vermelha, Earl

Bancroft persuaded him that there could be other rare red diamonds. My father said the earl showed him and the old miner Jose a map of a forgotten section of the mine, which had tunnels running deeper than a thousand metres.'

'But Earl Bancroft sold the mine soon after your father died following the accident. If there *had* been a map, Bancroft should have given it to the prospector who bought the mine from him. When we raised the money to buy Old Betsy from the prospector six years ago, you asked him about an old map but he denied any knowledge of one.'

Cruz shrugged. 'So maybe the earl kept the map a secret from the prospector. It wouldn't surprise me. I remember Henry Bancroft was a wily fox who looked after his own interests at the expense of the men he employed. The roof fall was a direct result of Bancroft's cost cutting and failure to adhere to safety procedures. When he sent my father into an area of the mine that he knew to be dangerous he effectively signed Papai's death warrant.'

Bitterness swept through Cruz as he thought

of the mining accident that had claimed his father's life. Ten years ago Vitor Delgado had been buried beneath tons of rock, but Cruz remembered it as if it had happened yesterday. Clawing at the rubble of the collapsed mine roof with his bare hands, choking on the thick dust as he had desperately tried to reach his father. It had been two days before they had brought Vitor to the surface—alive, but so severely injured that he had died from internal bleeding a few hours later.

Cruz closed his eyes and the years fell away. He was back in a hospital room, with the smell of disinfectant and the beep of the machine that was monitoring his father's failing heartbeat. His mother and sisters were sobbing.

'Don't try to speak, Papai. You need all your strength to get better.'

He had refused to believe Vitor would not recover even though the doctor had murmured that there was no hope. Cruz had put his face close to his father's and struggled to understand the injured man's incoherent mutterings.

'Earl Bancroft showed me a map of tunnels

dug many years ago. He believes there are red diamonds as big as the one I found deeper underground. Ask him, Cruz...ask him about the map...'

Even as he was dying Vitor had been obsessed with diamonds. Amongst miners it was known as diamond fever—the desperate lengths men would go to in their quest for the glittering gemstones that could make them rich.

For Cruz and Diego the dream had come true.

After his father died Cruz had become responsible for his mother and young sisters. Mining was the only job he knew and he worked in a coal mine where the filth and sweat and danger were at least repaid with good wages, which allowed him to pay for college evening classes.

Three years later, armed with a business degree, he got a job with a private bank and quickly proved his brilliance in the boardroom. Other people were surprised by his ruthless determination to succeed but they hadn't seen the things Cruz had witnessed in the *favela*: the violence of the drug gangs, the drive-by shootings. They had never felt hunger in their bellies, or fear, and they had no idea that Cruz sought success and money because he knew what it was like to have nothing.

He was offered a position on the bank's board of directors and bought his mother and sisters a house in an affluent part of the city. Cruz was on his way up and his family would never be hungry again. But he wanted more. He didn't want to work for the bank—he wanted to be one of its millionaire clients.

He remembered the Estrela Vermelha—the Red Star diamond his father had found in the Montes Claros mine. The diamond had an estimated value of several million dollars, but it had belonged to Earl Bancroft, not to Vitor. It was mine owners who got rich, not the men who crawled through tunnels and risked their lives laying explosives to break through solid rock. So Cruz took the biggest gamble of his life and he and Diego bought the mine that had once belonged to Earl Bancroft. The prospector who sold it to them thought they were crazy—he hadn't found diamonds of any significant value in the mine—but he understood that diamond fever could turn sane men mad.

Six months later, kimberlite rock containing diamonds estimated to be worth something in the region of four hundred million dollars was discovered in Old Betsy. Cruz became the most valued client of the bank where he had once worked, and he established a prestigious jewellery company, Delgado Diamonds. Diego invested in a gold mine as well as various other business ventures, but both men remembered what it was like to be poor and hungry and they gave financial support to a charity set up to help Brazil's street children.

'If Earl Bancroft had really believed there was a deeper mine, why would he have sold up? Why didn't he open up the tunnels shown on the map?' Diego demanded.

'Perhaps he kept the map as a form of insurance policy in case he needed money in the future. He knew that whoever owned the mine would be likely to pay a fortune for a map of a second mine with the potential of containing more diamonds.'

Diego frowned. 'Are you suggesting we should offer to buy the map from the earl?'

'The hell I am,' Cruz growled. 'Legally the map, if it exists—and I believe it does—belongs to us. Any documents pertaining to the mine are the property of whoever owns it. Bancroft should have given the map to the prospector, and in turn it should have come to us when we became the new owners of the mine.

'For the past five and a half years we have mined good quality diamonds, but now the supply is virtually exhausted. You're right—to continue mining Old Betsy makes no economic sense. But if there *is* a second mine then I want what is rightfully ours, and I intend to go to Eversleigh Hall in England and demand that Earl Bancroft hands over the map.'

Diego gave Cruz a speculative look. 'It's possible you'll meet Sabrina at Eversleigh Hall. How would you feel about seeing her again?'

Cruz gave a short laugh. 'After ten years I might not even recognise her. She was eighteen when she came to Brazil. I imagine she is married by now—no doubt to a duke or lord, or some other peer of the realm with an aristocratic pedigree as long as her own. The honourable Lady Sabrina made it clear that she didn't want a commoner for a husband,' he said sardonically.

Sabrina had definitely not wanted to marry a lowly miner who scraped a living crawling through tunnels beneath the ground like a worm, Cruz brooded. She had not even wanted their child—her lack of emotion after she had suffered a miscarriage proved that she had regarded their affair and her subsequent pregnancy as a mistake.

He recalled the first time he had set eyes on Sabrina Bancroft. She had arrived from England to visit her father, and Cruz, walking out of the mining office next to the earl's ranch house, had been arrested by the sight of her alighting from a taxi.

He had never seen a woman like her before, certainly not in the *favela*. With her pale, almost translucent skin and light blonde hair, she had looked ethereal, untouchable. Cruz had stared down at his blackened hands and felt conscious of the sweat stains on his shirt. But Lady Sabrina had barely glanced at him before she had turned her elegant head away. It had been as if he did not exist, as if he was so far beneath her that he simply did not register on her radar. As he'd watched her poised figure walk into the house, a hot flood of desire had swept through Cruz and he had vowed he would make the English rose notice him.

Cruz's mouth tightened into a hard line. He had made a fool of himself over Sabrina, but in his defence he had been far less cynical at twenty-four than he was a decade later. In the intervening years when he had rapidly ascended the world's rich list he had learned the games people played and it amused him that he could take his pick of any of the women who would once have dismissed him as worthless.

Sabrina had rejected him when he'd had nothing to offer her but his heart. It would be interesting to see her reaction to him now that he could afford to buy her precious Eversleigh Hall. Although Cruz knew it was highly unlikely that the Bancrofts' ancestral home would ever come onto the market. Sabrina had once explained that the stately house and surrounding estate in Surrey had been owned by her family for more than five hundred years, passed down through the generations from father to son. Her brother would one day inherit the house and the earldom.

The implication was that there were some things money could not buy, but Cruz did not believe that. In his experience everything had a price. He fully expected that Earl Bancroft would be willing to sell him the map of the secret mine if he offered enough money.

As for the possibility that he would meet Sabrina again, Cruz shrugged. He had not thought about her for years and he wasn't interested in the past. All he cared about was the future and claiming the map of the diamond mine that legally and morally belonged to him.

CHAPTER TWO

THROUGH THE LIBRARY window at Eversleigh Hall Cruz could see a half-naked woman dancing in the fish pond. Her gyrating body was illuminated by the lights blazing from every window in the house. Shouts of encouragement came from the group of young men standing on the lawn, swigging champagne from a bottle, before one of them jumped into the water and grabbed hold of the woman while his friends called out obscene suggestions.

Classy, Cruz thought sardonically. He had seen similar behaviour in the *favela* where he had spent most of his childhood, although the *putas*—the hookers—had been drunk on beer rather than Bollinger. For all the English aristocracy's wealth and privilege and their education at the finest schools, some of them were no more refined than the slum-dwellers from the poorest areas of Brazil.

His lip curled as he remembered an incident that had occurred at a high-society party he had attended in London a few days ago. The hosts, Lord and Lady Porchester, were 'old money' but in recent years crippling death duties and some diabolical business decisions had left the family fortune dwindling and they were desperately seeking investors to save their manufacturing company.

Cruz had been under no illusions about why he was an honoured guest. Porchester had sucked up to him all evening, but when Cruz had stepped outside onto the terrace for some fresh air he had been hidden in the shadows and had overheard his host discussing him with another guest.

'Delgado's a self-made millionaire from South America. Apparently he bought a diamond mine and struck lucky. Of course you can always pick out the nouveau riche by their lack of breeding.'

The two men had laughed and Cruz had

gritted his teeth and reminded himself that he would have the last laugh because money was money at the end of the day, and Porchester needed a loan. But Lord Porchester's meaning had been clear. It did not matter how many millions Cruz had in the bank, he would never be accepted by the social elite. Not that he gave a damn about other people's opinion of him, Cruz brooded. But he was determined to establish Delgado Diamonds as one of Europe's most exclusive jewellers and being regarded as an outsider by the aristocracy was a disadvantage.

Perhaps he should have accepted Porchester's daughter's unsubtle hints that she hoped he would take her to bed, he mused. If he was seen to be dating a lord's daughter it could open doors for him. Business relied on networking and making useful contacts. Unfortunately, the half an hour he had spent listening to Lisette Porchester gossiping about her 'Chelsea Set' friends had bored him rigid.

But there were plenty of other upper-class women he could choose from. Cruz knew it was not just his millionaire status that the opposite sex found attractive. Women were drawn to the sensual promise in his eyes and the athleticism of his muscular body. They called him a stud and he was happy to prove it. Since he was a youth, women had thrown themselves at him. Maybe that was why he found the cut and thrust of business so exciting—there was an element of risk and the possibility of failure that was never present in his numerous sex-without-strings affairs.

He turned away from the window, bored by the scene of drunken debauchery taking place on the lawn, and glanced around the library. Eversleigh Hall deserved its reputation as one of England's finest stately homes. From the outside the house was a gracious manor house, predominantly Georgian in style, although some of the original sixteenth-century building still remained. Inside, the impressive entrance hall and the library had a rather faded elegance about them—as if the house had been trapped in a time warp when grand country houses were run by dozens of staff.

The only member of staff Cruz had seen was the elderly butler who had admitted him into the house. He frowned. Had he imagined an odd expression had crossed the butler's face when he'd asked to see Earl Bancroft?

He wondered why the earl was hosting a party for guests who seemed to be barely out of high school. Perhaps the party was for Sabrina's younger brother, he mused. Tristan Bancroft must be in his early twenties now. Ten years ago Sabrina had used the excuse that she wanted to return to Eversleigh Hall because her kid brother needed her. The real reason, Cruz knew, was because she'd felt trapped in Brazil when she had been expecting his child. After she'd lost the baby she had rushed back to England and the privileged lifestyle she was used to.

His mind snapped back to the present as he noticed the door handle turn, and his jaw hardened at the prospect of meeting Earl Bancroft—the man he held responsible for his father's death.

The door opened and Cruz stiffened.

* * *

'It *is* you.' Shock stole Sabrina's breath and her voice emerged as a thread of sound. Cruz was instantly recognisable and yet he looked different from the man she had known ten years ago. Of course he was older, and the boyishly handsome features she remembered were harder, his face leaner, with slashing cheekbones and a chiselled jaw that gave him an uncompromising air of power and authority combined with devastating sensuality.

The curve of his lips was achingly familiar and memories of the feel of his mouth on hers flooded back. How could she remember his kiss so vividly after all this time? she wondered, dismayed by her reaction to him. She unconsciously flicked her tongue across her lower lip and saw his eyes narrow on the betraying gesture.

Cruz had always been able to decimate her equilibrium with one glittering glance from his olive-green eyes, Sabrina thought ruefully. She recalled the first time she had seen him in Brazil. Even as a young man, his body had been honed and muscular from working in the diamond mine. His jeans and shirt had been filthy, and when he'd taken his hat off, she had noticed that his black hair curling onto his brow was damp with sweat.

She had never met a man so overwhelmingly male before. The sheltered life she had led at Eversleigh Hall and at an all-girls boarding school had not prepared her for Cruz's smouldering sensuality. She'd taken one look at him and scorching heat had swept through her body. Disconcerted by her reaction, she had behaved with an uncharacteristic lack of manners and ignored him. But a few days later she had met him while she was out walking and he had told her that his name was Cruz Delgado before he'd pulled her into his arms and kissed her with a blazing passion that had set the pattern of their relationship.

For a moment Sabrina felt like a shy, unworldly eighteen-year-old again and she was tempted to run out of the library away from Cruz's brooding stare. She was twenty-eight, had a PhD and was highly regarded in her field of expertise in antique furniture restoration, she reminded herself. His unexpected appearance at Eversleigh Hall was undeniably a shock, but she assured herself that she was immune to his simmering sexual chemistry.

'Why are you here?'

She was thankful her voice sounded normal. But seeing him again brought back memories of her miscarriage just four and a half months into her pregnancy. She wondered if Cruz ever imagined what their son would be like if her pregnancy had gone to term. Did he sometimes picture, as she did, a strong-jawed, dark-haired boy with his father's green eyes, or perhaps his mother's grey ones? The raw pain that had torn her apart in the weeks and months after the miscarriage had faded with time, but there would always be a lingering ache in her heart for the child she had lost.

'I need to speak to your father.'

Fool, Sabrina berated herself, remembering that the butler had said Cruz had asked to see Earl Bancroft. The reason for his visit had nothing to do with her. He hadn't cared about her ten years ago. The only reason he had asked her to marry him was because he had wanted his child. But having witnessed her parents' disastrous marriage, Sabrina had been wary of making such a commitment. She had been sure Cruz did not love her and so she had turned him down.

Cruz did not look as though he was besieged by memories of the past. He was dressed in an impeccably tailored grey suit that moulded the lean lines of his body, and a white shirt that contrasted with his darkly tanned face. He looked the phenomenally successful multimillionaire businessman that she had read about in both the financial pages and the gossip columns of the newspapers. Yet beneath his air of suave sophistication she sensed there was still a wild, untameable quality about Cruz Delgado that had so intrigued her when they had been lovers.

Once again she felt the urge to flee from the library but she forced herself to walk into the room, closing the door behind her with a decisive click.

Cruz was standing behind the desk, his hawk-like features set in an arrogant expression as if he owned Eversleigh Hall, damn him. A memory slid into her mind of when she had been a little girl called into her father's study to explain some misdemeanour. Earl Bancroft had not been a particularly strict parent, more an uninterested one. He'd spent most of his time abroad and when Sabrina was a child her father had been a stranger who upset her mother and created a fraught tension in the house that disappeared when he went away again.

Lifting her chin, Sabrina walked around the desk to where Cruz was standing by the window, but she regretted her actions when she realised how close she was to him. She was sure it was not by accident that he'd moved his position slightly so that she was trapped between his powerful body and the desk. The musk of his sandalwood cologne was instantly familiar and she recognised the brand of aftershave she had given him as a present soon after she had given him her virginity. Had he deliberately worn that particular brand tonight to torment her?

Unwilling to meet his gaze, she glanced towards the window and made a choked sound when she saw what appeared to be a group orgy taking place on the lawn. 'For heaven's sake!' she muttered as she quickly twitched the curtains shut.

'Your friends are clearly enjoying themselves,' Cruz drawled.

'They're not my friends.' Sabrina could feel her face burning. She wasn't a prude but the behaviour going on—not to mention the amount of clothes coming off—in the garden was unacceptable.

'Are they your brother's friends?' Cruz was curious. 'Is it Tristan's party?'

'Tristan is away at university.' Thankfully her brother was nothing like Hugo Ffaulk and his ilk, Sabrina thought to herself. Tris knew that to fulfil his ambition of being an airline pilot he had to gain a first-class degree. Of course there was also the little matter of the one hundred thousand pounds required for the pilot training.

The merry-go-round of worries inside her head did another circuit. Somehow, she vowed, she would find the money for her brother to train for the career that he had dreamed of since he was a small boy.

'So, are those people your father's guests?'

Sabrina had no intention of telling Cruz that giving parties at Eversleigh Hall was a business venture. No one apart from her and the bank manager knew of the financial catastrophe that was looming over Eversleigh, and so far she had managed to keep the news that Earl Bancroft was missing out of the media.

'They are my guests, who I invited to my party,' she said stiffly. 'Some of them are just a little over-exuberant, that's all.'

Cruz gave her a sardonic look. 'I've heard gossip on the London social scene about the wild parties you throw at Eversleigh Hall. What does Earl Bancroft think about his stately home being overrun by upper-class yobs?'

'My father isn't here. He's away on a trip and I don't know when he'll be back. I'm sorry I can't be of more help.' She tried to step past him and gave a startled cry when he caught hold of her arm.

'That's it?' Cruz growled. 'I see you haven't changed in the past ten years, *gatinha*. You still think you can dismiss me as if I am dirt beneath your shoe.'

'Don't be ridiculous.' She tried to jerk her arm out of his grip. 'And don't call me that. I'm not your kitten.' Hearing him use the affectionate name he had called her when they had been lovers, in a sarcastic tone, hurt more than it had any right to.

His gravelly, sexy accent brought her skin out in goose bumps. She wanted to stop staring at him but she could not tear her eyes from the sculpted planes of his face and his sensual mouth. 'I never treated you like dirt,' she muttered, startled by the accusation. Surely she had made it embarrassingly obvious ten years ago that she'd worshipped the ground he walked on?

'The first time we saw each other you put your nose in the air and ignored me.'

She gave a shaky laugh. 'I was eighteen and painfully naïve. The nuns who taught at St Ursula's College for Ladies never explained about handsome men who could make a girl feel…' She broke off, flushing as Cruz's gaze narrowed on her face.

'Feel…what?' he demanded. Sabrina recognised the predatory gleam in his eyes and she instinctively backed away from him until her spine was jammed against the desk.

'You know how you made me feel.' She silently cursed the huskiness in her voice. 'And I didn't ignore you for long. You made sure of that.'

He'd had her in his bed within a week of her arrival in Brazil. Memories assailed her of blistering hot days when they'd had blisteringly exciting sex in the shade of the rubber trees, and sultry, steamy nights when Cruz had climbed up to her balcony at the ranch house and they'd made love beneath the stars.

The rasp of Cruz's breath warned her that he was also remembering their scorching passion. But sex was all they had shared, Sabrina thought. Their response to each other ten years ago had simply been a chemical reaction. Disturbingly, the mysterious alchemy of sexual attraction was at work again now. She could see it in the way his olive-green eyes had darkened so that they were almost black.

Her spine would be bruised from where she was pressing against the desk. She searched her mind for something to say to break the simmering tension in the room. 'Why do you want to see my father?'

'I believe he has something that belongs to me, and I want what is mine.'

Cruz stared at the stunning diamond pendant Sabrina was wearing around her neck. The Estrela Vermelha—the Red Star—was one of the largest red diamonds ever to have been found in Brazil. Cruz knew that diamonds could occur in a variety of colours, with red being the rarest. When his father had found the gem, the uncut, unpolished stone had not looked as though it was worth a fortune.

Earl Bancroft had had the stone triangular-cut, or trilliant-cut as it was known to gemologists. The red diamond had been set in a border of white diamonds and the contrast between the red and white sparkling gems was truly breathtaking. The pendant had never been for sale, but conservative estimates suggested it was worth well over a million pounds.

When Sabrina had entered the library Cruz had been so fixated on her that he had barely noticed the Estrela Vermelha, he acknowledged grimly. Her ruby-red dress was a perfect match for the red diamond nestling between her breasts. The silk jersey dress clung to every dip and curve of her slender figure and when she walked, the side split in the skirt parted to reveal one long, lissom leg.

The dress was overtly sexy, and with her pale blonde hair tumbling in silky, glossy waves around her shoulders Sabrina looked like every red-blooded male's fantasy, yet she still retained an air of elegance and refinement that spoke of her aristocratic bloodline.

A haze of jealousy clouded Cruz's mind as he wondered who Sabrina had dressed like a vamp for. He glanced down at her left hand and saw that it was ringless. So, it was likely that she was unmarried. Not that he gave a damn, he assured himself. Had she chosen to wear the scarlet dress to impress a lover? A vision sprang into his mind of Sabrina in the arms of another man. Why the hell did that make his blood boil? he asked himself impatiently.

He had been her first lover but he was damned sure he hadn't been her last—not when she had the body of Venus and a luscious mouth that simply begged to be kissed. Her lips were coated in a scarlet gloss that emphasised their sensual shape and her grey eyes were enhanced by a smoky shadow on her eyelids.

Cruz visualised the innocent girl he had known a decade ago. Sabrina had been an exceptionally pretty teenager, but now she was a stunningly beautiful woman, entirely aware of her sensuality and with the self-confidence to wear clothes that showed off her exquisite figure.

It was still there. He had not seen her for ten years, but one look was all it had taken to make him realise that he had never desired any woman as much as Sabrina Bancroft. Thinking of her family name reminded him of why he had come to Eversleigh and the hatred he felt for Earl Bancroft.

He reached out his hand and touched the Estrela Vermelha. The jewel was as cold and hard as his anger as he remembered his father's excitement when Vitor had discovered the rare diamond.

'It's likely that there are more red diamonds in the part of the mine where I found the first one. If I find more, Earl Bancroft has promised I will receive a share of their value.'

'Don't go back there, Papai,' Cruz had pleaded with his father. *'That part of the mine is dangerous. Some of the miners say that the roof supports aren't strong enough.'*

But Vitor had ignored him. *'I have to go back.'*

The earl had sent Vitor to search for more diamonds and had sent him to his death. Cruz still had nightmares about when he'd heard the incredible roaring noise of the mine roof collapsing as tons of rock had crashed down on his father and buried him alive.

He snatched his hand away from the Estrela Vermelha. 'Red is a fitting colour for a diamond which is stained with my father's blood.'

A shiver ran through Sabrina. She couldn't explain why she had never liked the Red Star diamond even though she admired its flawless beauty. The only reason she had worn it tonight was because she had wanted to impress the party guests. People booked parties at Eversleigh Hall because they liked the grandeur and history of the stately home, and they had no idea that, short of a miracle, the hall might soon have to be sold and would no longer be the ancestral home of the Bancroft family.

The dark red diamond was the colour of blood, but Cruz's words did not make any sense to Sabrina. 'What do you mean? What does your father have to do with the Red Star?'

'He found it, and it was his right to claim part of the value of the diamond. But he died before he received his percentage share. My father was killed doing your father's dirty work,' Cruz said harshly. 'Earl Bancroft sent him into the mine to search for more red diamonds. Your father has Vitor's blood on his hands and I have come to Eversleigh to demand compensation for my father's life.'

CHAPTER THREE

'I WANT YOU to leave.'

Sabrina whirled away from Cruz and faced him across the desk, breathing hard as she struggled to control her temper. 'How dare you turn up at Eversleigh uninvited and make a ridiculous accusation against my father, who isn't even here to defend himself?'

'He couldn't defend himself against the truth.' Cruz welcomed his anger as a distraction from the infuriating knowledge that when Sabrina had squeezed past him, her breasts had brushed against his chest and his body had reacted with humiliating predictability. His eyes were drawn to the low-cut neckline of her dress and the jerky rise and fall of her breasts. He pictured her naked beneath him, the erotic contrast of her milky pale body against his dark bronze skin, and he remembered her soft, kitten-like cries in the throes of orgasm.

Inferno! It was two months since he had dumped his last mistress and clearly he had gone too long without sex, he thought with savage self-derision. The purpose of his visit was to persuade Earl Bancroft to hand over the map of the abandoned mine, but all he could think of was how much he wanted to bend Sabrina over the desk and push her dress up to her waist, baring her silken thighs so that he could…

Ruthlessly he controlled his imagination but he could not control the painful throb of desire in his groin as he tried to focus on what she was saying.

'I didn't know your father had died.' She hesitated. 'I'm sorry… I know how close you were to him. But I don't believe my father was responsible. How could he have had anything to do with Vitor's death?'

'When my father found the Estrela Vermelha, the earl sent him back to an area of the mine that he knew was unsafe to look for more diamonds.' Cruz's jaw hardened. 'Don't pretend you didn't know. Bancroft must have told you about the accident at the mine even if he failed to admit his culpability for what happened.'

'My father didn't confide in me,' Sabrina admitted. 'We've never been close. I grew up at Eversleigh, but my father had inherited land and the diamond mine in Brazil from an uncle and he spent months at a time abroad. I visited him when I was eighteen, which is when I met you, but when I came back to England I had little contact with him.'

She fell silent, remembering the bleakest period of her life when she had hidden away at Eversleigh like a wounded animal. There had been no one she could talk to about the miscarriage. Four years earlier, when she had been fourteen, her mother had walked out of her marriage to Earl Bancroft and abandoned her children for her lover, and Sabrina had learned a valuable lesson—that she could not trust anyone and she had to rely on herself.

When she'd fallen pregnant by Cruz in Brazil she had told her father about her pregnancy. Typically he had said little then, or later, when she'd informed him that she had lost the baby. His only comment had been that he thought she had made the right decision to return to England and take up the university place she had deferred.

The earl had paid an unexpected visit to Eversleigh Hall during the summer ten years ago, Sabrina suddenly recalled. Her father had been in a strange mood and even more uncommunicative than usual, but he had made the surprising announcement that he intended to sell his diamond mine. He'd made no mention of Vitor Delgado's fatal accident, or of Cruz, and Sabrina's pride had refused to allow her to ask about him.

She had spent her first weeks back at Eversleigh hoping that Cruz would come after her, but as time went by she had been forced to accept that he wasn't coming and he did not care about her. Now she'd learned that he had suffered a terrible tragedy soon after she had returned home. Following his father's death his focus would understandably have been on taking care of his mother and much younger twin sisters.

She studied his face and noticed the fine lines around his eyes and deep grooves on either side of his mouth that had not been there ten years ago. He had idolised his father and would have felt Vitor's loss deeply. She felt a faint tug on her heart. 'When did the accident at the mine happen?'

'Three weeks after you had left me and returned to England. It was the worst time of my life. First you lost our baby and then I lost my father.'

Sabrina stiffened. 'An estimated one in seven pregnancies ends in miscarriage,' she said huskily, repeating what numerous medical experts had told her when she had sought an answer as to why she had lost her baby. 'We were unlucky.'

'Perhaps it was simply bad luck.' Cruz's tone was devoid of any emotion, but Sabrina was convinced she had heard criticism in his voice. She curled her hands into tight balls until her fingernails cut into her palms.

'Riding my horse did not cause me to miscarry,' she said in a low tone. 'I was seventeen weeks into my pregnancy and beyond the risk period of the first three months. The doctor said I was not to blame.' But she had always blamed herself, she acknowledged bleakly, and she had suspected that Cruz thought she'd been irresponsible to have gone riding.

'If you'd had your way, you would have wrapped me in cotton wool for nine months,' she burst out.

His over-the-top concern had been for the baby, not for her. Every day, when Cruz had gone to work at the mine he had left her under the watchful and disapproving eyes of his mother. Sabrina had felt lonely and bored in Brazil. She'd been delighted at her three-month scan when the doctor had said that her pregnancy was progressing well and there was no reason why she should not do the things she normally did. She had thought it would be safe to take her horse for a gentle ride, aware that her mother had ridden during both of her pregnancies.

Cruz's chiselled features were impassive. 'There is no point in dragging up the past.'

His harsh voice jerked Sabrina from her painful memories. Her long lashes swept down, but not before Cruz glimpsed raw emotion in her grey eyes that shocked him. Ten years ago her lack of emotion after the miscarriage had made him realise that she had not wanted their child, and her hurried departure from Brazil had proved that she did not have any feelings for him.

His jaw hardened and he told himself he must have imagined the pained expression in her eyes. 'You said that the earl is away, but I need to speak to him urgently. I assume you keep in contact with him by phone or email?'

She shook her head. 'All I know is that he is probably in Africa. He has investments in a couple of mines there, and he often takes trips into remote areas to investigate new mining opportunities.'

Everything she had said was true, Sabrina assured herself. Her father often went abroad on what he called his adventures. But he had never stayed out of contact for this long. She had last spoken to Earl Bancroft when he had called her from a town somewhere in Guinea, but, after eighteen months when nothing had been seen or heard of him, Sabrina was seriously concerned for her father's safety.

'I'm afraid my father is incommunicado at the moment,' she murmured.

There was something odd about the situation, Cruz mused. Something Sabrina wasn't telling him. With difficulty he restrained his impatience.

'Well, if I can't talk to Earl Bancroft perhaps you will be able to help me. I believe your father has some information about the Montes Claros diamond mine. Before my father died, the earl showed Vitor a map of an abandoned section of the mine. The map is the legal property of the mine owner. You might be aware that I bought the mine six years ago, which means that the map belongs to me.'

Sabrina shrugged. 'I don't know anything about a map. I told you my father rarely confides in me about his business dealings.'

A vague memory pushed into her mind. At the time she hadn't paid much attention to the incident, but Cruz's words made her wonder about her father's curious behaviour when she had walked into his study and found him looking at a document spread out on his desk. Earl Bancroft had snatched up the piece of paper before Sabrina had got a clear glimpse of it and thrust it into an envelope.

'This is my pension fund for when I retire,' he'd said, laughing. *'It's much safer to keep it hidden here at Eversleigh than in a bank.'*

'Why is the map important?' she asked Cruz curiously.

'I believe it shows a section of the mine that was dug many years ago.' He shrugged. 'There may be nothing down there, but the Estrela Vermelha was found in the deepest section of where we currently operate and it's possible that there are other diamonds in the abandoned mine.' Cruz's eyes raked Sabrina's face and she quickly dropped her gaze.

'Did your father ever show you a map?'

'No,' she said truthfully.

'Do you know where he might have put a map? Does he have a safe where he keeps important documents?'

She shook her head. 'He wouldn't need to lock things in a safe. Eversleigh Hall had dozens of secret places to hide valuables—and people, come to that. Many old English houses have secret chambers and priest holes, which were built hundreds of years ago when Catholic priests were persecuted,' she explained. 'For instance, one of the wooden panels in this room conceals a secret cupboard. My father knows the location of all the hiding places at the hall.'

'And do you also know where the secret chambers are?'

'I know where some are, but not all of them. Even if I knew every hiding place I wouldn't show you their location without my father's permission.'

Sabrina felt a sense of loyalty towards Earl Bancroft despite the fact that they had never shared a close emotional bond. Since her father's mysterious disappearance she had realised that she loved him. She looked at Cruz steadily. 'If you are really the rightful owner of the map then I'm sure my father would have given it to you when you took over the mine.'

'Don't pretend to be naïve,' Cruz growled. 'I won't go so far as to say that Earl Bancroft is a crook, but some of his business dealings are decidedly shady.'

'How dare you—?'

'I worked for him,' Cruz cut her off impatiently. 'I saw how your father ignored safety regulations in the mine to save money.'

Sabrina's eyes flashed with anger. 'My father isn't here to defend himself and I only have your word on what happened.'

'And of course you, with your aristocratic title and privileged lifestyle, would not believe the word of someone who grew up in dire poverty in a slum,' Cruz said sardonically. 'You always thought I was beneath you, didn't you, *princesa*?'

'That's not true.' During their affair she'd hated it when he had mockingly called her princess to emphasise that they came from different ends of the social spectrum. 'I never cared about where you came from, or that you didn't have much money.'

He gave a harsh laugh. 'You made it obvious that you were desperate to return to Eversleigh Hall.' He glanced around the comfortable library with its shelves of books from floor to ceiling and plush velvet curtains hanging at the windows. 'I can understand why you hated living in a cramped miner's cottage with a corrugated-iron roof, when you were used to living in a grand mansion.'

'I didn't hate the cottage, but we lived there with your parents and your mother never made me feel welcome.' Sabrina saw disbelief in Cruz's eyes and knew it would be pointless trying to convince him that she hadn't minded the basic living accommodation in Brazil. But his mother's unfriendliness had been hard to cope with. Ana-Maria Delgado had patently adored her son, and perhaps in Cruz's mother's eyes no woman would be good enough for him, Sabrina mused.

As Cruz had said, there was no point in dragging up the past. It had all happened a long time ago and their lives had moved on. Ironically their fortunes had reversed for Cruz was now a millionaire, while since her father's disappearance she had spent every last penny she had paying for the upkeep of Eversleigh Hall, and she and the house were practically bankrupt.

'Some things about you haven't changed. Your eyes still darken to the colour of storm clouds when you lie.'

Cruz's deep voice jolted Sabrina from her thoughts and she tensed as he walked around the desk and stood unsettlingly close to her.

'Ten years ago when I asked you if you were happy to live in Brazil with me and have my child, you assured me that you were, but your eyes were as dark as pewter and revealed the truth—that you wanted to return to Eversleigh Hall.'

She flushed guiltily and looked away from his intent gaze that seemed to bore into her skull and read her thoughts. 'I missed my brother,' she said quietly. 'Tristan was just a kid of eleven. After my mother left we had become very close and I was worried about him living here with just a nanny to take care of him.'

'I don't believe that concern for your brother was the only reason for your eagerness to leave Brazil, any more than I believe you are unable to contact Earl Bancroft if you wish to,' he said sardonically. 'I also think you know more about the map than you have admitted.'

She had forgotten how tall he was, Sabrina thought, feeling a frisson of panic when she realised that he had moved imperceptibly closer to her. She could see the shadow of black chest hairs beneath his crisp white shirt and the faint delineation of his powerful abdominal muscles. Seductive images taunted her subconscious: Cruz's naked, bronzed body pressed against hers, hard against soft, dark against her whiteness. She visualised him pulling her down on top of him, his strong arms holding her as he guided her onto his erect shaft while she slowly took him inside her.

Heat coursed through her veins. The few lovers she'd had in the past ten years had never evoked more than her mild interest, and sex had been disappointing. But to her shame she was bombarded by memories of Cruz's magnificent virility and she was aware of a betraying dampness between her legs.

Anger was her only defence against the insidious ache of longing in the pit of her stomach. 'I've told you I know nothing about a map and it's not my problem if you refuse to believe me.'

Even though she was wearing four-inch heels she had to tilt her head to look at his face. Ten years ago she hadn't stood a chance against him, she thought bitterly, feeling an ache in her heart for the innocent girl she had once been who had looked forward to going to university. Cruz had taken one look at her and decided he wanted her, but within months of the start of their affair she had been pregnant and facing a very different life in Brazil from the one she had been used to in England.

If he had loved her she would have coped with her new lifestyle, she thought sadly. But when her pregnancy had been confirmed Cruz's desire for her had died and it had quickly become clear that they had nothing between them to sustain a relationship.

She felt the ache of tears at the back of her throat. It was silly to cry for a lost love that in truth had only ever been an illusion, she reminded herself.

'I want you to leave,' she said tautly. She frowned when he made no response, merely raised his dark eyebrows and surveyed her with an arrogance that made her seethe.

'I suppose you think I should be intimidated by your air of menace. Perhaps you think you can force the whereabouts of the map out of me, but I have plenty of staff in the house.' She mentally crossed her fingers behind her back as she thought of John and his wife, Mary. The butler and housekeeper were the only remaining staff living at Eversleigh and were past retirement age. 'If you lay a finger on me I'll scream.'

She spun on her heels, intending to march over to the door, but his hand shot out and he caught hold of her arm and jerked her round to face him.

'I don't think force will be necessary to persuade you to give me what I want,' he murmured.

Sabrina's stomach muscles clenched as his sensuous, molten-syrup voice tugged on her senses. Time seemed to be suspended and her breath was trapped in her lungs. Her eyes widened as she watched his dark head descend and she realised that he was going to kiss her. He wouldn't dare, she assured herself. But this was Cruz Delgado—a man who would dare to make a deal with the devil if he believed the odds were in his favour.

'I warned you, I'll scream.' It was melodramatic, but she felt melodramatic, damn it! She gasped as he pulled her against him and she felt the heat from his body melting her bones.

He gave a wolfish smile. 'Perhaps you will. I remember how you used to scream with pleasure and claw me with your sharp nails when you came, *gatinha*.'

'Cruz—for God's sake!' In desperation she thumped his shoulder with her fist, but her blows had as much effect as a mosquito landing on a rhino's hide.

'You are so goddamned beautiful,' Cruz said harshly. He could not resist her and he was shamed by his weakness. If he kissed her, perhaps the fire blazing inside him would cool and he would be released from this mad desire that made his muscles taut and his heart pound. He clamped one arm around her waist and slid his other hand into her hair and up to clasp her nape as his mouth swooped down to capture hers.

Cruz's lips were hard, demanding, as he forced Sabrina to accept the mastery of his kiss. She was unprepared for the savage hunger that ripped through her. She was transported back in time to when she had been eighteen; a girl on the brink of womanhood, a virgin who had given not only her body but her heart and her soul to Cruz. It had taken her ten long years to reclaim them.

The memory of how badly he had hurt her gave her the strength to fight him. But he remembered how to pleasure her and he knew how to undermine her defences with the bold sweep of his tongue as he traced the shape of her lips before thrusting between them to explore the moist interior of her mouth.

Sabrina felt herself tremble and knew Cruz must sense she was close to total capitulation. But rather than increase the pressure of his mouth he softened the kiss and took little sips from her lips, butterfly soft and so utterly beguiling that she sagged against him and kissed him with a sweetness and curiously evocative innocence that caused Cruz to abruptly lift his head.

Deus! He had not come to Eversleigh Hall with the intention of making love to Sabrina. His eyes shot to the big mahogany desk and for a few seconds he was tempted to sacrifice his hope of finding the map, and probably his sanity, he acknowledged derisively, to satisfy the rampant desire raging through his veins.

He had not expected to feel this overpowering attraction to a woman he had known briefly when she had been a girl. Their affair had lasted for less than a year and after she had returned to England he had determinedly put her out of his mind. When he had arrived at Eversleigh Hall this evening he had assumed he would be immune to Sabrina Bancroft. The reckless craving that consumed him was a humiliating reminder of his weakness ten years ago when he had fallen under her spell after one glance from her storm-grey eyes.

Right now, Sabrina's eyes had softened to the colour of woodsmoke, the colour of her desire; Cruz remembered that sensual look and felt his body tighten in response. He swore silently to himself. He had been a fool once, but he would not make the same mistake a second time.

His mouth curled into an insolent smile. 'Your willingness to co-operate is encouraging. All I want now is the map, and I will leave you to enjoy your *party*.'

The mockery in Cruz's voice ripped apart the seductive web he had woven around Sabrina. She pulled out of his arms, hot-faced and trembling with anger. It was bad enough that he believed she actually *liked* playing hostess to Hugo Ffaulks and his bunch of immature friends. But worse was the realisation that Cruz had only kissed her in order to make her lower her guard so that she would give him a map that he was convinced was hidden somewhere at Eversleigh Hall.

Oh, God! What was wrong with her? She hadn't seen him for ten years, but within ten minutes of meeting him again she had all but invited him to hitch up her skirt and take her right there on the desk. Erotic images swirled in her head and her shame was compounded by Cruz's husky chuckle that told her he had seen her gaze flick towards the desk. Without pausing to think, she lifted her hand and struck his cheek with a resounding crack that shattered the silence in the library. *'Get out.'*

His eyes glittered. 'I don't advise you try that again,' he said in a measured tone that despite its softness sent a shiver down Sabrina's spine.

'Just…go,' she whispered.

When he'd driven from London to Surrey, Cruz had not anticipated making the return journey without the map in his possession. But his visit to Eversleigh Hall had not gone to plan.

He grimaced at the understatement. Now he was at an impasse. Either Sabrina genuinely did not know about the map that Earl Bancroft had shown his father, or she was refusing to tell him where the earl kept it.

A sudden loud crash from outside the library broke the stand-off, and with a muttered oath Sabrina hurried across the room and opened the door.

'John,' she called to the butler, 'what on earth was that noise?'

'I'm afraid it was Sir Reginald, Miss Sabrina. Some of the guests knocked him over.'

Bemused, Cruz followed Sabrina into the hall and saw the suit of armour that he had noticed when he'd arrived at the house lying in pieces on the parquet floor. A group of young men who were clearly the worse for drink were attempting to fit the pieces back together. One of them staggered towards Sabrina.

'Sorry about your knight, Sab…rina,' he slurred. 'I want you to know that this is the best birthday party ever.'

'I'm glad you are enjoying yourself.' Sabrina

spoke crisply as she tried to sidestep around Hugo Ffaulks, but his reactions were quicker than she'd anticipated and he slid his arms around her waist.

'I enjoyed you coming to my bedroom this morning. Will you wake me up the same way tomorrow morning, Sabrina?'

Sabrina missed the cynical expression on Cruz's face. 'You can have breakfast in bed tomorrow if you wish, Hugo.' She struggled to hide her impatience as she reminded herself that the money his parents had paid for the party would cover the hall's outstanding electricity bill.

Still trying to extricate herself from the young man, she glanced along the hall and saw Cruz by the front door. She flushed when he deliberately dropped his gaze to Hugo's hands on her bottom.

'My apologies for disturbing you,' he said mockingly. 'Have fun for the rest of the night.'

Damn him to hell! Sabrina thought furiously as she watched him stride out of the house. She wrenched herself free from Hugo. She couldn't understand her burning desire to run after Cruz and slap the arrogant smile off his face. Usually she was mild natured, but he made her feel so angry that her body was actually shaking, and, when she glanced down, the sight of her pebble-hard nipples jutting beneath her dress was humiliating evidence that it was not only anger that Cruz aroused in her.

When he'd kissed her she had felt alive, truly alive, for the first time in ten years. Oh, she was safe from falling in love with him. She'd have to be certifiable to make that mistake again, but during those moments of passion in the library she had wanted him so badly that even now her breasts ached and she could still taste him on her lips.

She would have to get herself under control before she saw him again. And she was in no doubt that she *would* see him again. She knew from bitter experience that when Cruz wanted something he would not rest until he had it in his possession.

Ten years ago he had wanted her. Now he wanted a map that he insisted her father had hidden at Eversleigh Hall. She was certain that Cruz would be back, but next time she would be prepared for his sizzling sexual charisma and she would not melt the moment he looked at her, she promised herself.

CHAPTER FOUR

THE EXCEPTIONALLY SMOOTH single-malt whisky served at the Earl's Head loosened tongues and encouraged local gossip, Cruz discovered. Following his unproductive visit to Eversleigh Hall he had returned to the village pub, where he had earlier booked a room for the night, and ordered a double measure of Scotch with a splash of water, no ice.

'There's no better cure for life's problems than a drop of amber nectar,' the old man sitting at the bar—a farmhand, Cruz guessed from his rough clothes—commented.

'Too true,' Cruz muttered as he pushed his empty glass towards the barman and asked for a refill, plus the same for his companion. Two-thirds of the bottle of whisky later, Cruz had learned some interesting facts about the Bancroft family, including that the pub had been named after one of the current earl's ancestors, who had been accused of fraud and treachery during the reign of Elizabeth I and beheaded for his crimes.

Treachery clearly ran in the family genes, Cruz thought bitterly. Henry Bancroft had cheated his father out of his rightful share of the Estrela Vermelha diamond, and tonight Sabrina had denied any knowledge of the map of the abandoned mine. But Cruz was certain she was lying. When he had questioned her she had hesitated for a fraction too long and her eyes had darkened to the colour of wet slate.

He drained the whisky in his glass and nodded to the barman to refill it. What could he do? He could hardly shake the truth out of her, he brooded. Somehow he needed to gain access to Eversleigh Hall so that he could search for the map that it seemed likely her father had hidden in one of the house's secret places.

He thought of his meeting with Sabrina and felt furious with himself. It had been a mistake to kiss her, but he had been unable to resist her cool beauty and he despised himself for his weakness. Although it had not been all one-sided, he consoled himself. Sabrina's ardent response proved that she still wanted him and the knowledge was a useful weapon that he would be a fool not to use.

Cruz pulled himself from his thoughts when he realised that the farmhand was speaking.

'I wouldn't be surprised if Lady Sabrina up at the hall didn't try to forget her problems with the help of a bottle of highland malt.'

'What kind of problems?' Cruz asked curiously.

'Money.' The farmhand shook his head. 'The estate has become more and more run-down since her father took over from the old earl many years ago. Henry Bancroft never spent much time at Eversleigh. He was always going abroad for business reasons. It's said that he trades in diamonds, but no one has seen the earl for well over a year and there's a rumour in the village that his daughter has reported his disappearance to the police.'

Cruz remembered Sabrina's curious statement—*my father is incommunicado at the moment*.

'My guess is Lady Sabrina is struggling to cope with running the house and estate.' The farmhand downed his whisky and allowed the generous stranger who was such a good listener to fill his glass again. 'I used to do a bit of work up at the hall myself, but all the staff have been laid off, apart from old John Boyd and his wife who have been in service there for as long as anyone can remember, and some young girl who looks after the stables.' He sighed. 'The trouble is these old country houses are expensive to maintain. It'll be a shame if Eversleigh is sold.'

'There may not be anything left of it to sell,' the barman said as he put down the phone and came over to them. 'That was Miss Bancroft. There's a fire up at the hall, and she phoned to ask if some of her guests can spend the night at the pub.' As he finished speaking the loud wail of a fire engine's siren sounded outside on the main road.

How bitterly ironic it would be if the house

went up in flames before he'd had a chance to find the map of the diamond mine, Cruz thought grimly. Aware that he was over the alcohol limit to drive, he said urgently to the barman, 'Can you call a taxi to take me to Eversleigh Hall?'

'I'm glad to report that the fire is under control. The blaze was almost certainly caused by a smouldering cigarette dropped onto a carpet or chair,' the fire officer explained to Sabrina. 'I understand there was a party taking place here tonight. Perhaps one of the guests drank too much and fell asleep holding a lit cigarette.'

'I'd asked people not to smoke in the house.' She grimaced. 'I can't believe how quickly the fire spread and how much damage it has caused. It looks as though most of the top floor of the east wing and the roof have been completely destroyed.'

The fireman glanced up at the dark sky as rain began to fall. 'I suggest you call a local building firm to come and rig up tarpaulins so that the damaged part of the house will be protected from the weather until you can see if any of the furnishings are salvageable.' He gave her a sympathetic smile. 'I imagine some of the paintings are originals and irreplaceable, but at least they'll be covered by your contents insurance.'

Sabrina felt a sensation like concrete solidifying in the pit of her stomach as the fireman's words sank in. Three months ago she'd had to cancel the contents insurance policy on Eversleigh Hall because she had been unable to afford the premium. It had been a difficult decision but there had been other more urgent bills to pay for, such as a new boiler for the central heating system that had packed up on the coldest day of the winter. Since then she had been meaning to renew the policy but unforgivably it had slipped her mind.

At least Hugo Ffaulks and his friends had been safely evacuated and had gone to stay at hotels in the village. But the fire spelled the end of her fledgling party business at Eversleigh Hall, and probably her family's association with their ancestral home, Sabrina thought bleakly.

She could not even afford to pay for tarpaulins to cover the damaged section of the house, let alone the building and restoration costs.

She heard a car door slam, and her heart crashed against her ribs when she saw Cruz striding towards her.

'Sabrina.' His husky accent lingered on each syllable of her name. He splashed through a puddle, uncaring that filthy black water stained his pale grey trousers. 'Are you all right?' he demanded, clasping her shoulders.

'I'm fine.' Her voice was muffled against his chest as he pulled her towards him, and for a few seconds she closed her eyes and allowed his strength and vitality to seep into her.

'It looks as though only the newer part of the house was affected by the fire, and luckily the older and more historically important section is undamaged,' he commented.

Of course the house and, more importantly, the map that he believed was hidden somewhere inside were Cruz's only concern—not her, Sabrina told herself as she stepped away from him and ruthlessly crushed her pang of hurt.

She frowned when she saw a ginger figure flash past and bolt into the fire-damaged part of the house. '*George!* Come back.'

'Who is George?' Cruz found he was talking to himself as Sabrina tore across the lawn before disappearing into the fire-blackened house.

'George, where are you, sweetheart?' Sabrina called, vainly trying to peer through the blackness. The part of the house where the fire had done most damage was known as the annexe. It had been built in the early nineteen hundreds, and, as Cruz had commented, was of less historic importance than the main house. The flames had been extinguished but the rooms were still full of thick smoke that made Sabrina's eyes sting. *'George.'*

'Is George the guy who was looking forward to being woken by you in the morning?' Cruz's deep voice cut through the darkness and Sabrina jumped when he appeared at her side.

'What…?' Comprehension dawned as she remembered that when Cruz had paid his first visit to Eversleigh Hall earlier in the evening, the party had been in full swing. 'No,' she said distractedly, 'that was Hugo. George is—'

'Another of your juvenile lovers?' Cruz suggested. 'How many do you have? You should not play with boys, *gatinha.* You need a man to satisfy you.'

'How would you know what I need?' She bristled at his outrageous arrogance.

'I know that the boyfriend I saw you with at the party is not strong enough for you. On the surface you are the cool and composed lady of the manor, but beneath your serene smile there is, not ice, but heat and simmering sensuality. You need a man who can tame your fiery temperament and who would be prepared to put you across his knee if necessary.'

Sabrina's choking fit had nothing to do with the smoky atmosphere. 'You are the most chauvinistic *dinosaur* I've ever had the misfortune to meet,' she spluttered. 'We haven't seen each other for ten years and you have no idea what I want.'

'You want me,' he said with infuriating self-assurance. 'Did you think I didn't feel the quickening of your heartbeat when I kissed you earlier, or that I did not notice the flush of sexual desire that stained your creamy skin so prettily?' His voice deepened and his husky accent caused the hairs on the back of Sabrina's neck to stand on end. 'It's still there, Sabrina, and we both recognised it in the library. I could have had you on the desk and you would have been with me all the way. I bet you have never met another man who excites you as much as I do.'

Sabrina was thankful that the darkness hid the wave of heat she felt spreading across her cheeks. 'This is an utterly ridiculous conversation and an even more ridiculous place to be having it.' She swung away from Cruz and yelped as she stubbed her toe on a door frame. 'Damn it, I can't see a thing.' She blinked as a light suddenly flared and she saw that it came from Cruz's mobile phone. 'There's George,' she cried as she glimpsed the glitter of green eyes.

'George is a *cat*?' Cruz swore. 'I can't believe you risked your safety for a cat.'

'He was probably terrified by the fire and

he's looking for somewhere to hide. Quick—grab him before he runs off.' Sabrina heard a yowl, followed by a torrent of Portuguese that she guessed from Cruz's tone it was lucky she did not understand. 'Have you got him?'

'It would be more to the point to say that he has got me,' Cruz muttered as he viewed the ball of orange fur that had attached its teeth to his hand with considerable dislike.

'Oh, my poor darling.' Sabrina's soft-as-butter voice went some way to soothing Cruz's damaged pride, until he realised that she was speaking to the cat. The animal responded to the sound of his mistress and released its grip on Cruz's flesh before leaping into Sabrina's arms.

'I don't think he's injured,' she said as she carried George outside and inspected him anxiously.

'Lucky cat,' Cruz muttered, wrapping a handkerchief around his hand to try and staunch the blood pouring from the teeth marks left by the creature from hell.

'Thank you for rescuing him. Oh…' Sabrina

was shocked to see blood pouring from Cruz's hand. 'George only bites when he's upset. It just goes to show how traumatised he must have been, poor angel.' Seeing Cruz's glowering expression, she added hurriedly, 'You had better come into the house and let me clean the wound.'

The main part of the house, including the kitchen, had not suffered any fire damage. Sabrina set George down on the floor and fed him a handful of cat treats before she took the first-aid box from a cupboard. 'Wash the bite area thoroughly,' she instructed. 'Cats have a high level of bacteria in their mouths and bites can easily become infected.'

'Wonderful,' Cruz said drily. As he held his hand under the tap he gave George a dark look and was fairly certain than the deep sound coming from the cat's throat was not a friendly purr. He turned his attention to the breakfast trays set out on the counter. 'Had you planned to serve your guests breakfast in their rooms?' He counted the trays. 'It must take you all morning.'

'I have John, the butler, to help me, although the arthritis in his knees means he can't manage the rooms on the top floors. A girl from the village comes to help on party weekends. Breakfast in bed is part of the party package offered at Eversleigh.'

Sabrina saw the puzzled look Cruz gave her and bit her lip. The shock of the fire was sinking in and she was struggling to contain her emotions. 'You may as well know the truth as it will be public knowledge soon,' she said heavily. 'I can't afford to pay for the upkeep of the house and estate and I might have to sell up. It's been on the cards for a while, but tonight's fire means that selling Eversleigh Hall looks unavoidable.' The words sounded like a death knell, and misery settled heavily in the pit of Sabrina's stomach.

Cruz dried his hand on the paper towel that Sabrina gave him and allowed her to apply antiseptic solution to the bite wound. 'I assume the maintenance costs of a huge mansion are expensive.' He recalled his conversation with the farmhand in the pub. 'Has your father run out of money?'

'There is money in his account but I can no longer access it to pay the hall's bills since—' Sabrina hesitated '—since Dad disappeared. He's been missing for over a year and his bank accounts and assets have been frozen. I've employed a missing persons' agency to search for him but so far they've found no trace of him. If he isn't found after a number of years, he will be presumed dead, but in the meantime I've used all my savings and spent everything I earn on the house and, to put it bluntly, I'm broke.'

'I imagine a house this size must be worth a lot of money,' Cruz said casually.

'The house and estate, which consists of three hundred acres of prime Surrey land, have been valued at ten million pounds.'

Cruz's brows rose. That much! Eversleigh Hall was worth more than he had expected. It had occurred to him that he could buy the house so that he would have the opportunity to look for the map of the diamond mine. But a house as old as Eversleigh was bound to be a money pit, and there was a chance that the map did not exist. He was a gambler but he wasn't a fool.

'It will probably take some time to find a buyer,' he commented, thinking that in the meantime he needed to persuade Sabrina to allow him to search the house for the map. 'Not everyone can afford, or would want the responsibility of owning, a historic stately home.'

'I already have a buyer lined up. A hotel chain approached me a few months ago and made an offer for the estate. The Excelsior Group plan to build a golf course in the grounds and turn the house into a luxury golf and spa resort.'

Her shoulders slumped. 'Once I give the go-ahead for the sale it should only take a matter of weeks. Sometimes I've even wondered if I would be happier to be free of the worry of trying to maintain the estate. But this is my home and I have happy memories of living here with my mother before she left us. My father was never interested in Eversleigh but I always hoped that one day Tristan would run the place properly.'

Cruz frowned at the unwelcome news that the house could be sold so quickly. 'You said your father's assets are frozen because he is officially registered as a missing person. Surely Eversleigh Hall is listed as one of his assets, so how can it be sold without his knowledge or permission?'

'The house is owned by a group of trustees made up of Dad, me and my brother. Only two of us need to agree to the sale.'

'And Tristan is in agreement?'

'Tris is unaware of the financial situation,' she admitted heavily. 'I've tried to spare him the worry because he is studying for his final exams at university. He'll be upset to lose our ancestral home, but he's a realist and he'll understand that we have no choice but to let Eversleigh go.'

Sabrina was shocked to feel tears sting her eyes. She rarely cried, but the impact the fire would have on her life, if—as it seemed almost certain—she would have to leave the only home she had ever known, was starting to truly sink in. Feeling as vulnerable as she did, the last thing she felt able to cope with was Cruz.

Sabrina used the excuse of putting the first-aid box back in the cupboard to move away from Cruz. Being so close attending to his injured hand, she was supremely conscious of his lean, muscular body. Vivid memories rose to the surface, the feel of him on top of her, his weight pressing her into the mattress as he thrust into her over and over again.

Just thinking about him making love to her induced a molten sensation between her legs, and a quick glance downwards showed the outline of her nipples was clearly visible. She reminded herself that the peach silk robe she had pulled on over her matching nightdress when the fire alarm had sounded was perfectly respectable, but she was aware of Cruz's intent scrutiny and fought the urge to cross her arms over her breasts. It was imperative that he leave before she made an idiot of herself, and she walked over to the kitchen door, hoping he would take the hint and follow her.

He was unfairly gorgeous, she thought as she

took advantage of him looking at his phone to study his chiselled features. Wealth and success had given him an air of sophistication that he had not had ten years ago, although he had never lacked self-confidence, she acknowledged. She flushed when he suddenly looked up and caught her staring at him.

'It's late,' she said abruptly, glancing at the kitchen clock. 'I'm sure you can appreciate that it has been a stressful night. I want to go to bed so I'll have to ask you to leave.'

Cruz flashed a smile that stole her breath. 'Not a chance.'

She stiffened. 'What do you mean?'

'I mean that I am not going to allow you to stay here on your own while the house is unsecured. Every burglar and criminal in the area will have heard about the fire. They won't even have to break in—they can simply walk into the fire-damaged part of the building and access the rest of the house, including your bedroom.'

'Rubbish! You can't tell me what you'll *allow* me to do.' Sabrina's temper simmered. 'Anyway, there is very little crime in the village, and the local police constable said he will post one of his officers at the front gate tonight.' She placed her hands on her hips when Cruz did not move off the kitchen stool where he was sitting. 'I'm not going to argue with you.'

'Good idea,' he said blandly. 'Save your breath, *gatinha*, and show me to a spare bedroom.'

He slid off the stool and walked towards her, his eyes glittering with a fierce possessiveness that touched something deep inside Sabrina. Despite his size he moved with a noiseless grace and the predatory intent of a panther stalking its prey. 'Unless you would prefer me to share your room?' He stopped in front of her and ran his finger lightly down her cheek. The caress was as soft as a butterfly's wing brushing against her skin, yet her senses leapt and she felt as if he had branded her with his touch. 'Although I can't guarantee that either of us would get much sleep,' he murmured.

She swallowed hard, fighting the treacherous longing of her body. *Why not forget her worries for one night and lose herself in the guar-*

anteed sensual pleasure of making love with Cruz? whispered the voice of temptation in her head. But all he was offering was sex, she reminded herself. It hadn't been enough for her ten years ago, and she sensed it would not be enough now.

'You are unbelievable,' she told him tightly.

He grinned. 'So I've been told.'

Sabrina recalled the recent stories she had read in the newspapers about the hotshot Brazilian diamond tycoon who had taken the London social scene by storm and seemed to be intent on sleeping with every beautiful blonde he met. A sharp barb of jealousy stabbed her through the heart. To disguise her swift intake of breath she swung round and marched out of the kitchen door, aware, because she was so intensely aware of Cruz, that he followed her across the hall and up the stairs to the second floor. Frustration surged through her that she could not make him leave, but she recognised the determined gleam in his eyes and knew that she would lose an argument and probably her dignity in the process.

'You can use the bedroom at the far end of the corridor,' she told him in an emotionless voice, and did not glance at him as she walked swiftly along the hallway towards her room on the opposite side of the house.

But the trauma of the fire, the likelihood that she would have to sell her home, and more shockingly the images in her mind of Cruz naked in bed just down the corridor, kept her awake until the pearl-grey glimmer of dawn peeped through the chink in the curtains.

Eversleigh Hall had never looked more beautiful, Sabrina thought the next morning. She had ridden Monty up to the North Downs Way, classed as an area of outstanding natural beauty, and from her viewpoint the fire-damaged section of the house was hidden. In the early morning sunshine the sandstone brickwork gleamed palely gold, and she could see the elegant knot garden, the tall poplar trees and the deep blue of the lake.

Her heart ached. How could she bear to part from the place that meant so much to her?

How could she end the Bancroft family's five-hundred-year ownership of the hall? But what choice did she have? She had run out of money and ideas, and her hopes that her father would be found alive and well were fading.

Monty pawed the ground restlessly, bored by the prolonged inactivity. Sabrina patted his neck. 'Come on, boy, let's go home,' she said in a choked voice. The woeful state of her finances meant that selling her horse seemed unavoidable.

Cruz was waiting for her in the stable yard. It was the first time since he'd come back into her life that Sabrina had seen him in daylight and her heart slammed against her ribs as her eyes were drawn to his black hair gleaming like raw silk in the sunshine.

She dismounted and let Monty loose in the paddock while she dealt with Cruz.

'You're up early,' he commented. 'I thought you might be tired after the events of last night.'

'Nothing happened between us…' She broke off and flushed hotly. 'Oh, you meant the fire.' Idiot, Sabrina told herself furiously. She didn't want Cruz to guess that she had been kept awake for most of the night by erotic fantasies of him making love to her. 'Dawn is my favourite time to ride, when the sun is pale pink in the sky and the dew on the leaves sparkles like diamonds.'

Outwardly, Sabrina was the archetypal ice princess, Cruz thought as he studied her cool beauty. Her pale blonde hair was tied in a long plait that fell to halfway down her back and her intelligent grey eyes surveyed him with an unflattering lack of interest. Only the faint tremor of her sensual mouth and the delicate rose flush on her porcelain skin gave a clue to her inner fire.

His arousal was instant and uncomfortably hard. Damn her witchery, he thought grimly. He could not take his eyes off her. Last night she had looked glamorous in her scarlet evening gown, and when he had returned to the house after hearing about the fire he had been turned on by the sight of her in a silky robe. This morning she was no less sexy wearing jodhpurs that fitted her like a second skin, teamed with a soft grey cashmere sweater that echoed the colour of her eyes and clung with loving attention to the firm swell of her breasts. The sound of her cut-glass accent catapulted Cruz back to the present.

'I trust you slept well?'

He recalled the previous night tossing and turning beneath the sheets and sweating like a teenage boy with a surfeit of hormones. 'I didn't stir all night,' he lied. 'I have to go back to London, but I've arranged for a local building firm to come to the house and make it secure.'

'That's unnecessary. There's no need for you to get involved,' she said stiffly.

'You have no money,' Cruz reminded her. His eyes rested on the stubborn set of her lips and he wondered how she would react if he were to crush her mouth beneath his and kiss her into submission. She would probably slap his face again, he decided with a mixture of amusement and reluctant admiration, remembering her explosion of temper in the library the previous evening.

'On the subject of your financial difficulties—I have a proposition to discuss with you. Not now.' He did not give her a chance to speak. 'I'm due at a meeting at eleven.' He handed her a business card. 'This is my London address. Meet me there at six tonight if you are interested in finding out how I might be able to help you.'

Pride snapped Sabrina's spine straight. 'I don't need your help.'

'Don't be late.' Cruz swung his jacket over his shoulder, but instead of walking away he stepped closer to her and wrapped her long plait around his hand. 'And wear your hair loose tonight, Sabrina, to please me.'

Sabrina's chest heaved as she sucked oxygen into her lungs. 'Why on earth would I want to please you?'

He grinned before dropping a brief, hard kiss on her lips. 'Because you need salvation, *querida*, and I might just be the answer to your prayers.'

CHAPTER FIVE

SHE WOULD RATHER walk barefoot over hot coals than meet Cruz at his London home, Sabrina thought grimly as she watched the taxi that had come to collect him drive away from the house. As for him being an answer to her prayers! She gave a snort of derision.

Her heart lurched when in the distance she saw a car turn into the main gates of Eversleigh Hall and she thought for a moment that Cruz was coming back. The sound of a blowing exhaust pipe was a clue to the visitor's identity.

'Tris!' Sabrina forgot her worries as she gave a cry of pleasure and ran to meet her brother. 'I wasn't expecting you this weekend,' she said when Tristan uncoiled his lanky frame from his old car. She inspected him with loving eyes. 'I'm sure you've grown.'

He grinned. 'When are you going to stop

saying that? I'm not a kid any more, I'm twenty-one.'

Tristan might be a good six inches taller than her, but he would always be her little brother and she would probably always try to mother him, Sabrina thought ruefully. She had taken on the role when their mother had left. Tris had only been seven. *'When is Mother coming back?'* he'd asked tearfully as they had stood at the nursery window and watched Lorna Bancroft drive away from Eversleigh.

Fourteen-year-old Sabrina had swallowed hard. *'She isn't. But we'll visit her at her new home in France in the summer holidays.'*

'But who will look after me for the rest of the time? Father is always going away, and I don't like the new nanny.'

'I will,' she had promised her brother. *'I'll always take care of you.'*

Cruz had not understood how much she had missed her brother. She had rushed back to Eversleigh Hall after the miscarriage because it was where she felt most secure. Tris had been her only source of comfort in those dark days when she had grieved for her baby. Having lost her own child, she had poured her maternal feelings onto her brother, and, even though he was now a strapping six-footer about to graduate from university, Sabrina still felt protective of him.

'What the hell happened to the hall?' Tristan's shocked voice pulled Sabrina's mind from the past. She followed his gaze to the burnt-out wing of the house and quickly sought to reassure him.

'There was a fire, but fortunately only the annexe was affected.'

Her brother gave her a worried look. 'You're all right? What about John and Mary?'

'No one was hurt.'

Tristan slung his arm around her shoulders. 'Well, that's the main thing. As long as you're okay, the damage can be repaired, and the insurance will cover the cost of rebuilding.'

Sabrina's heart sank. 'Tris, I need to talk to you about Eversleigh.'

He gave her another of his quick smiles. 'Let me tell you my news first, before I burst. I've passed the selection process to be a commercial pilot and been offered a place at an aviation school that provides airline-pilot training.'

'Oh, Tris, that's fantastic.'

'Of course, I'll need to get a first-class degree, but I'm on track to do that. The training is expensive though. I've been careful with my allowance, but I can't afford the flight school's fees. Dad promised he would invest in my career. Have you heard from the old man lately? I'll need the money soon so that I can start the training programme in the summer.'

Tristan was looking up at the burnt-out roof of the annexe and did not see Sabrina's troubled expression. She had not wanted to worry her brother while he was taking his final exams and had played down their father's disappearance, saying that Earl Bancroft was on an extended trip abroad. She couldn't keep the truth from Tristan for much longer, she realised, but she was certainly not going to ruin his excitement at being accepted for pilot training by revealing that there was no money to pay for it. This was it—she'd have to sell Eversleigh. It was the only way that would allow Tris to fulfil his boyhood ambition, the only way to raise the aviation school's fees. Wasn't it?

She remembered Cruz's parting comment.

I might just be the answer to your prayers.

She'd have to be desperate to turn to him for help. But she *was* desperate, she acknowledged grimly. What was Cruz's proposition that might help her? Was it a way to keep Eversleigh Hall and pay for Tristan's pilot tuition? Would it do any harm to find out?

Lost in her thoughts, she followed Tristan into the house and forced a smile when he put his hands on her waist and swung her round.

'Every time I come home I realise how much I love Eversleigh,' Tris said softly. 'I plan to have a career as a pilot, but one day I'll become the next Earl Bancroft and I'll settle here and take care of the place properly. After all, the estate is our heritage and it's my duty to look after it for future generations.'

Sabrina's heart clenched. Tristan's words echoed her own sentiments about Eversleigh. They were guardians of the historic house and she could not bring herself to tell her brother that they might be forced to sell it to a hotel chain. Ironically, if the estate was sold, there would be plenty of money to pay for Tristan's pilot training. If only her father would reappear, Eversleigh would be saved and she might even be able to get on with her own life without the burden of responsibility and worry that had haunted her for months.

Tristan stayed for lunch before driving back to university. 'You said you wanted to discuss something about Eversleigh,' he remembered as he was leaving.

'It's not important. Concentrate on your exams,' Sabrina told him. She lifted her face so that he could kiss her cheek and recalled how when he was a young boy she had often leaned down to kiss him and ruffle his hair. She loved her brother dearly and would do anything for him—even if it meant asking Cruz Delgado, the man who had once broken her heart, for help.

Cruz sipped his vodka martini and savoured the hit of alcohol at the back of his throat. He glanced at his watch—not the first time he had done so in the past half an hour—and gave a wry grimace. He did not usually drink this early in the day but he was annoyed to admit that he felt tense, wondering if Sabrina would arrive.

He looked out of the window of his serviced penthouse apartment opposite Kensington Palace. In the distance he could see the Serpentine Lake in Hyde Park sparkling in the clear light of the spring evening. The street below was lined with exclusive top-of-the-range cars. This was the most affluent part of London and the five-star hotels and chic boutiques were as discreetly elegant as their high-class clientele.

Kensington was a long way from the *favela* in Belo Horizonte, but in his dreams Cruz still walked the labyrinth of narrow alleyways that stank of rotting rubbish. A few times he had seen a body lying in the gutter, a victim of warring drugs gangs, or maybe just a poor fool who had been in the wrong place at the wrong time. He had learned from a young age to look over his shoulder and check around every corner before stepping out. Fear and hunger had been his constant companions.

His thoughts returned to Sabrina. Would she turn up tonight, lured by his hint that he could help with her financial problems? His jaw hardened. He was a gambler and his instincts for a sure bet told him she would come because she would do anything to safeguard her beloved Eversleigh Hall.

But would she agree to his ultimatum? His lip curled into a cynical smile. Sabrina would be a fool to refuse him. This afternoon, he'd discovered just how close Eversleigh was to bankruptcy because Earl Bancroft had bled the estate and used the money to fund his trips abroad and invest in numerous ill-advised business ventures. Coldness gripped Cruz's heart and he felt a sense of satisfaction that once he had been reliant on Earl Bancroft to pay his wages but in a reversal of fortune Sabrina would have to come to him for help to save her family home. The shift of power intrigued him and he wondered how she would react to him knowing that he had the upper hand. Surely the ice princess would have thawed—if she came?

He took another sip of his drink and stiffened when he heard the muted peal of the doorbell followed by the low murmur of voices as the butler invited the visitor into the apartment. Cruz recognised the cultured feminine tones and a ripple of anticipation ran through him. He swung round from the window as the sitting-room door opened and the butler ushered Sabrina into the room.

Most women who wanted something from him—and that was most women, he thought sardonically—would have dressed seductively in sexy, revealing clothes. Sabrina's plain black dress with its demure neckline and three-quarter-length sleeves was starkly simple, but as Cruz studied her he realised that the dress was exquisitely tailored to show off her slim figure. The silky material flowed over her body, moulding her high, firm breasts and following the contours of her narrow waist and hips.

He lowered his gaze to her legs encased in sheer hose and her black stiletto shoes that emphasised the shapely curve of her calves, before he lifted his eyes to her fine-boned face, beautifully made up and with the merest touch of pale pink gloss on her lips. The double string of pearls around her neck shimmered with a soft sheen that reflected her creamy skin and her pale blonde hair was swept up into a businesslike chignon. Sabrina looked what she was, a member of the English aristocracy with an impeccable pedigree; elegant, refined—untouchable.

For a moment Cruz was a young man again, a poor miner from a *favela,* entranced by an English rose but knowing she was out of his reach. Sabrina had been his once, he reminded himself. Ten years ago he hadn't been able to forget the difference in their social status. Now he was determined that she would be his again, but things were different. He was Sabrina's equal. He had made his fortune but she had lost hers and she needed his help. This time when they became lovers he would be in control and Sabrina would have to play by his rules, he decided as he strolled towards her.

* * *

The muted click of the door signalled to Sabrina that the butler had left the room and she was alone with Cruz. She was aware of her heart thudding hard beneath her ribs and fought the panicky feeling that made her want to run out of his apartment. She was not Cruz's prisoner, she reminded herself, she was his guest and she could leave whenever she chose.

She was well acquainted with Kensington and had frequently shopped at the exclusive boutiques, but since her father's disappearance her life had changed dramatically. A year ago she would have travelled up to town in the Bentley driven by the chauffeur. Now the Bentley was in the garage waiting to be auctioned, the chauffeur had a new employer, and she hadn't dared splash out on a taxi and had caught the Tube across London to Cruz's luxurious apartment. But she did not care about the loss of the little luxuries she had been used to. All she cared about was saving Eversleigh and helping her brother fulfil his dream of being a pilot.

She watched Cruz walk towards her and drew

a swift breath as she acknowledged how handsome he was. His black trousers were superbly tailored and his pale blue silk shirt was open at the throat to reveal his darkly tanned skin. Sabrina noticed a flash of gold on his wrist and recognised his watch was an exclusive and exorbitantly expensive brand.

The situation felt surreal. It was hard to believe that the suave, sophisticated man standing in front of her was the poor miner who had been her first lover ten years ago. In Brazil, the only clothes she had seen Cruz wear were ripped jeans and tee shirts, but she hadn't been bothered by his lack of money. She had fallen in love with his olive-green eyes and his wide smile, his springy, silky black hair that curled onto his brow and his fit, muscular body that he had used with dedicated skill to ensure her pleasure before he had taken his own.

Memories of him making love to her bombarded her mind and she quickly lowered her lashes to hide her thoughts from him, but she could not control the betraying thud of her pulse at the base of her throat when Cruz lifted his hand and removed the clip from her chignon so that her hair unravelled and fell in a heavy swathe down her back.

He met her fulminating look with a bland smile. 'You need my help and I suggest you drop your defiance,' he drawled. 'Your hair is like silk.' He wrapped a few strands around his finger. 'Always wear it loose when you are with me.'

She longed to tell him to go to hell, but the memory of her brother's excitement when he'd announced that he had been accepted for pilot training made her take a deep breath and she schooled her features into an expression of cool composure. 'What is your proposition that you invited me here to discuss?'

'All in good time,' Cruz said urbanely as he strolled over to the bar. 'Would you like some champagne?'

It might calm her nerves, Sabrina decided as she accepted the long-stemmed glass Cruz offered her. She noted that the champagne was an excellent vintage and once again she felt a sense of surrealism that the Cruz she had known ten years ago had drunk beer from a bottle, but now he seemed completely at ease with his millionaire lifestyle.

He waited for her to sit down before he lowered his tall frame onto the sofa facing her and stretched his arm along the backrest. The action caused his shirt to tighten across his chest so that Sabrina could see the delineation of his pectoral muscles. Although he presumably no longer worked down mines his physique was even more toned and powerfully muscular than when he had been a young man. Images filled her mind of his naked, bronzed body and she licked her suddenly dry lips and took a gulp of champagne.

'I have shown the top gemologist at my jewellery company Delgado Diamonds some photographs of the Estrela Vermelha,' Cruz said. 'He estimates its value to be in the region of one and a half million pounds, but of course he will need to assess the diamond properly and I suggest that you have your own independent valuation carried out.'

Sabrina wondered where the conversation

was leading. 'It was valued at one point four million pounds for insurance purposes. But why are you interested in what the diamond is worth?'

'Because I want it, and I am prepared to buy it from you.' Cruz's expression hardened. 'I wish to give my mother the Estrela Vermelha as tribute to my father. Vitor wanted to give his family the chance of a better life away from the slums, but in doing so he lost his own life and was cruelly snatched from my mother, sisters and I.'

The sudden huskiness in his voice evoked an ache of sympathy in Sabrina and without thinking she leant forwards to put a comforting hand on Cruz's knee, before it occurred to her that she was the daughter of the man he blamed for his father's death and perhaps he hated her as much as he hated Earl Bancroft. Flushing, she shoved her hand into her lap, and in the tense silence she brooded on Cruz's offer to buy the diamond. Her disappointment was acute even though she had told herself not to get her hopes up. She had clung to the possibility of a respite for Eversleigh, but now she knew there was none and it was hard to bear.

'I can't sell you the red diamond,' she said flatly. 'My father is its registered owner and it is listed as one of his personal assets, which, as I have already explained, I am unable to use as a means of raising capital.'

So that was that. She put her glass down on the coffee table in front of her, gathered her handbag and stood up. 'I'm truly sorry about your father's accident,' she blurted. 'I wish I could sell you the diamond, but I can't and I have nothing else to offer you.'

'That's not quite true.' A curious nuance in Cruz's voice made Sabrina hesitate as she was about to walk over to the door. 'There is something else I want and I am willing to pay the same amount that I offered for the Estrela Vermelha.'

She turned to look at him, her finely arched brows drawn together in a frown. 'I've told you I have nothing, apart from Eversleigh Hall.'

He stood up and towered over her. He appeared relaxed but his eyes glittered with a fierce gleam that caused Sabrina's heart to slam against her ribs. 'I don't want an ancient pile of bricks. I want you, Sabrina.'

Shock rendered her silent for several seconds as she registered his words and absorbed their meaning. She stiffened as he trailed his eyes over her in a frank appraisal, as if he was mentally stripping her naked, she thought furiously. Even worse was her treacherous body's reaction to the sensual promise in Cruz's gaze. Her breasts ached with a delicious heaviness and every nerve-ending on her skin tingled.

I want you. No doubt he had said those words to the countless attractive blondes he was reputed to have had affairs with. The tabloids were full of stories about the hotshot Brazilian diamond tycoon's playboy lifestyle, and she would just be another notch on his bedpost, Sabrina realised bitterly. But she would be an expensive notch because Cruz was offering to pay her to sleep with him as if she was a hooker he had picked up off the streets. His suggestion was deeply insulting and she hated him for it, but she despised her body even more for responding to his smouldering sensuality.

Her heart ached as she remembered a much younger Cruz with smiling eyes, who had taken her virginity so tenderly and whispered soft words in Portuguese while he'd made love to her with sweet passion. She had loved him so much, but by offering to buy her sexual favours he had given her the ultimate proof that she had never meant anything to him.

Years of practice at disguising her feelings meant that her expression revealed nothing of her thoughts. 'Am I to understand that you are offering to pay me a million pounds to have sex with you?' she said coldly. 'Did you really think that I would *prostitute* myself? Let me make something absolutely clear. I would *never* demean myself by sharing your bed, however much money you offered me. You have become a wealthy man, but you need to learn that there are some things your money can't buy.'

Ice replaced the fire in Cruz's blood as he met Sabrina's disdainful grey gaze, and he struggled to control his anger. Once more, he recalled Lord Porchester's party.

'Delgado's a self-made millionaire...you can always pick out the nouveau riche by their lack of breeding.'

He jerked his thoughts back to the present. For a few moments Sabrina's disdain had made him feel unworthy and ashamed of his poor background. *Deus*, he should not feel ashamed because he hadn't been born with a silver spoon in his mouth. He owed his fortune partly to luck at discovering top-grade diamonds in the Montes Claros mine, but for years before that he had slogged his guts out to provide for his mother and sisters.

His jaw hardened. How dared Sabrina, who had only ever known a life of privilege and luxury, tell him in her cultured accent that she would not demean herself to have sex with him? In fact she had jumped to the wrong conclusion when she had accused him of offering to pay her for sex. What he had been going to suggest was that she would allow him to move into Eversleigh Hall so that he could search for the map of the diamond mine and in return he would pay for the cost of the repairs to the annexe and the ongoing expenses of maintaining the estate.

It was true he had hoped that if he and Sabrina lived under the same roof they might rekindle their affair. He desired her more than any other woman, and he knew she wanted him. God knew he had enough experience of women to be able to recognise the telltale signs of attraction. He had been prepared to woo Sabrina. He'd been looking forward to an enjoyable chase before she finally and inevitably succumbed to the chemistry that existed between them.

But she had scraped his pride raw and now the rules of the game had changed. She might look at him as if he were something unpleasant on the sole of her shoe, but he would have her in his bed and he would make her beg for him to possess her and give her more pleasure than she had ever known with any other man, Cruz vowed to himself.

* * *

She had to get out of Cruz's apartment immediately, Sabrina decided, before her tenuous hold on her emotions cracked and she did something unforgivably stupid like agree to any demands he made if only he would take her in his arms.

Without saying another word she walked swiftly across the room, but her sense of relief as she gripped the door handle turned to panic when Cruz caught hold of her arm and swung her round to face him.

She flashed him a steely glare, which he returned with an amused smile.

'I'm fascinated by the contrasts in your personality,' he drawled. 'As I've said before, you give the impression of being cool and controlled, but beneath your ice there is fire and passion and a depth of sensuality I've never known in any other woman.'

She did not want to hear about his other women. 'Take your hands off me.'

'Don't push my patience, *gatinha*. I am your only hope of saving your precious Eversleigh

Hall. I know you have applied to various banks for a loan and been turned down.'

Her temper simmered. 'How can you possibly know personal information about me?'

'Information isn't difficult to obtain if you pay the right people.' When she did not reply, he continued in a hard voice. 'What I'm offering is a simple exchange. My money, which you can spend on maintaining your family's ancestral home, and in return you will be my mistress for six months.'

'Six *months*!'

He shrugged. 'That's somewhere in the region of one hundred and eighty nights, for which you'll get paid one and a half million pounds. Not a bad return surely, *querida*?'

The Portuguese endearment transported Sabrina back in time to when Cruz had called her darling as if he had meant it. She searched his hard-boned features for any sign of softening but found none. 'Why do you want to humiliate me?' she whispered. 'Once we created a child together and you asked me to be your wife. Did our relationship ten years ago mean so little to you?'

'It meant little to you,' he said harshly. 'If it had meant anything you would have accepted my marriage proposal. But you would have preferred our child to have been born illegitimate than to marry a man you considered below your social class.'

'That's not true.' She was shocked by his accusation. 'I never thought you were below me. My decision not to marry you was because I had seen how unhappy my parents' marriage had been. My mother once told me that the only reason she had married my father was because she had fallen pregnant with me. I didn't want history to repeat itself.'

'The argument about marriage became obsolete after you suffered a miscarriage,' Cruz said flatly.

His comment confirmed what Sabrina had already guessed—that he had only asked her to marry him because he had wanted his child.

'I'll find a way to save Eversleigh that doesn't

entail having to have sex with you,' she told him fiercely.

'If I only wanted sex I could obtain it for a lot less than I am willing to pay you.'

She frowned. 'What else do you think I can provide?'

'Class,' he said succinctly.

'You've got a hang-up about class. A person's position in society doesn't matter.'

'It shouldn't matter, but it does.' Cruz's expression became cynical. 'It doesn't matter how much money I have in the bank, or how many yachts or penthouse apartments I can afford to buy. I will always be regarded as an outsider by the aristocracy because I wasn't educated at one of the top public schools and I can't trace my family tree back hundreds of years to show that my ancestors were linked to royalty like you can, Lady Bancroft.'

Sabrina gave him an impatient look. 'Having a title means very little these days.'

'It is an invaluable commodity in business, and especially to a business like Delgado Diamonds. My jewellery company is aimed at the top end of the market. My boutiques in Dubai, Paris and Rome have received acclaim, but the success of the company will be measured by sales at the flagship premises that I am about to open on Bond Street.'

'What do your business plans have to do with me?'

'Delgado Diamonds needs to attract a certain class of wealthy clientele, people who demand exceptional design and craftsmanship and will think nothing of spending thousands of pounds on an item of jewellery. The old-school aristocracy won't be interested in a jewellery company owned by an ex-miner who grew up in a slum in South America,' Cruz said bluntly. 'But if I am seen to be in a relationship with an earl's daughter who belongs to one of the oldest and most prestigious families in England, I'll become acceptable in high society, particularly as I intend to move into Eversleigh Hall with you. It will be the perfect opportunity for me to search for the map of the diamond mine that belongs to me.'

Cruz's lips curled into a sardonic smile as he

studied Sabrina's stunned expression. He lifted his hand and slowly ran his knuckles down her cheek and the white column of her throat and was exultant when he felt the frantic beat of her pulse. Despite her proud words he knew she would be his whenever he chose to take her. He was tempted to sweep her into his arms and carry her through to the bedroom so that their bodies could communicate on a fundamental level that did not require words.

The shadows in her grey eyes stopped him and he felt a faint tug of regret that they were on opposing sides of a battlefield. It was safer that way, he reminded himself. She was the only woman who had ever made him lose control, unmanned him with her sweetness and fire and mind-blowing passion, but he would not succumb to such craven weakness again.

'As well as having been born into a high-ranking family you are a respected historian specialising in antique furniture restoration, and, according to my private investigator, you have undertaken commissions at the Wallace Collection and the Victoria and Albert Museum. You are also a well-known patron of the arts and no society dinner party is complete without your name on the guest list.'

Sabrina drew a sharp breath. 'I can't believe you instructed someone to pry into my private life.'

He shrugged. 'The first rule of business is to thoroughly research the subject you are interested in, and, in this instance, I am interested in you.'

'Because of my so-called pedigree,' she snapped.

'You belong to the rarefied world of the English upper class. I can get sex anywhere,' Cruz stated coolly. 'What I desire from you, Sabrina, is your heritage and breeding. You will be my very public mistress and your connections to the aristocracy will open doors that would otherwise be closed to me.'

Sabrina held her breath as he trailed his knuckles over the upper swell of her breast and she felt her nipples pucker in anticipation of his touch. She jerked away from him and this time he did not prevent her from opening the door. 'Hell will freeze over first,' she told him grimly.

His mocking voice followed her down the hallway. 'I'll give you three days to come to me, *querida*. If I haven't heard from you by seven p.m. on Tuesday evening I will withdraw my offer and you will have lost your chance to save Eversleigh Hall from the developers.'

CHAPTER SIX

THERE WAS NOT a chance in hell that she would agree to Cruz's outrageous ultimatum, Sabrina thought angrily, when she arrived back at Eversleigh Hall. But she had to face the stark truth that she could no longer afford to keep the house and estate, especially as it seemed increasingly possible that her father might not be found.

The fire and the huge costs of repairing the annexe had made a bad situation even worse. The best thing she could do would be to sell Eversleigh to the Excelsior hotel chain. But she hadn't discussed it with Tristan yet, she argued with herself. She had hoped he could finish his exams before she broke the news that he might lose his home and heritage. In retrospect she knew she should have explained the situation to her brother months ago, but she had spent so many years caring for him after their parents' divorce and she still felt an instinctive need to try to protect him.

Ten years ago Cruz had not understood how worried she had felt about leaving her brother in England. He had accused her of wanting to return to her comfortable life at Eversleigh Hall, but, in the end, the arguments about where their baby would be born had been immaterial. Seventeen weeks into her pregnancy she had started to bleed heavily. Cruz's mother had driven her to the hospital because Cruz had been at work at the mine. By the time he had arrived at her bedside Sabrina had had to tell him that he was no longer going to be a father.

She had called her baby boy Luiz. A lump formed in her throat. Memories of the miscarriage had become less painful over time, but seeing Cruz again had brought it all back. She had been consumed by grief and guilt that the miscarriage was somehow her fault and had sought refuge at Eversleigh, resuming her role of parent to her brother as a way of helping her through the mourning process. For a long time she had hoped that Cruz would come to her and they would be able to grieve for their child together. But weeks and months had passed and she had not heard from him.

He had not wanted her once she was no longer carrying his child. He did not want her for herself now, Sabrina thought bitterly. He had made the insulting proposition that she could sell her body to him for the price of the red diamond. But even more insulting—and hurtful, damn it—was his admission that he had only chosen her to be his mistress rather than any of the blonde bimbos who flocked round him because of her breeding. He made her sound like a prize heifer!

As she passed the portraits hanging in the hall she paused by a painting of the daughter of a previous Earl Bancroft who had lived in the time of the notorious womaniser King Charles II. According to a family story retold through generations, Lady Henrietta had become a mistress of the king in return for him settling the huge debts her father had left when he died, thereby saving Eversleigh Hall from being sold and allowing Henrietta's younger brother to inherit the earldom and the estate.

Heaven help her. Perhaps whoredom was in her genes! Sabrina thought wryly.

Her mind kept on replaying her confrontation with Cruz and she had no appetite for the chicken salad the housekeeper had prepared for her. The TV failed to hold her attention, and she switched it off and went into her studio where she carried out restoration work on Eversleigh Hall's collection of antique furniture. But the detailed work of applying gold leaf to a Georgian cabinet that she had spent weeks restoring seemed a waste of time when there was a strong chance that the cabinet would have to be sold with the house.

In the library that her father had used as his study she began to search the drawers in the desk for the map Cruz had spoken of. It was unlikely that Earl Bancroft would have put something that he presumably valued highly in such an obvious place, but it had occurred to her that if she could find the map it was possible she could make a deal with Cruz.

Half an hour later, Sabrina had found nothing of interest apart from a couple more bills that she had been unaware of and that required paying immediately. Lying at the bottom of the last drawer she opened was a photograph of her parents on their wedding day. The cracked glass in the frame summed up her parents' marriage, she mused. Neither her mother nor father looked happy, but the old earl, Sabrina's grandfather, had insisted that his grandchild could not be born out of wedlock.

Her parents must have had a brief spell of marital harmony which had resulted in Tristan being born. But her father had soon grown bored of family life. Deserted by her husband for long periods, Lorna Bancroft had started an affair with a groom who worked at the Eversleigh estate.

As Sabrina replaced the photo in the drawer she mused that her parents' shotgun marriage had not been a good advertisement for wedded bliss. It was why she'd turned down Cruz's proposal, but she was surprised to learn he believed she'd refused because she'd thought he wasn't good enough for her.

Was her rejection of him years ago the real reason for his humiliating proposition that she could sell herself to him for the price of the red diamond? Back then, Cruz had been far more bothered than she had by what he had perceived as the difference in their social status and he'd refused to move to England and live at Eversleigh Hall with her in case he was labelled a gold-digger. Now that their financial situations were reversed and she could be seen as a gold-digger if she accepted money from Cruz, Sabrina had a new insight into how he must have felt when he had been a poor miner in a relationship with an earl's daughter.

She still had not called! Cruz checked his phone for new messages and felt a mixture of frustration and disbelief when Sabrina's name did not appear in his in-box.

He put his phone back down on the boardroom table and forced himself to concentrate on the details of the launch party for his new Bond

Street store that the event planner was explaining. Opening a Delgado Diamonds shop in the heart of London was the biggest gamble he had ever taken. As he'd explained to Sabrina, the success or failure of his whole jewellery company depended on whether the new store would attract the super-rich clientele who could afford to live and shop in exclusive Mayfair.

This was what he had been working towards for years, ever since he had created Delgado Diamonds. For months he had focused on little else, but for the past three days he had barely given a thought to his business expansion plans, his mind preoccupied with Sabrina. Not just his mind, Cruz acknowledged with savage self-contempt, recalling his erotic fantasies about her.

He had been certain she would accept his offer of financial help in return for becoming his mistress. She had reacted furiously when he had set out his terms, but he had given her a few days for her temper to cool and he'd been convinced that she would agree to his demands, which would allow her to safeguard Eversleigh

Hall. He knew how much the stately home meant to her and he could not understand why she was delaying her inevitable capitulation.

He glanced at his watch. Five hours left until the deadline he had given her expired. Would she come to him? His gut twisted as he faced the possibility that she would thwart him. He drummed his fingertips on the polished table and acknowledged that he couldn't take the risk that Sabrina might decide to sell Eversleigh Hall to a hotel chain and deny him the chance to search for the map of the diamond mine.

'Would you like to accompany me to the party venue to make sure you are happy with the arrangements, Mr Delgado?'

Cruz forced himself to concentrate on the matter at hand and smiled at the young woman from Party Perfect who was organising the launch party.

'I'm sure that you and your team have done an excellent job, Miss Simms.' He stood up and slipped his phone into his jacket pocket. 'Something urgent has come up and I'll be busy for the rest of the afternoon, but I'll be back in time for the party at eight this evening.'

It was the third day! Sabrina could not dismiss the thought and she was finding it hard to concentrate on the intricate restoration work on the Georgian cabinet. She now understood why Cruz had given her an ultimatum of seven o'clock this evening to decide if she would sell herself to him. Several of the daily newspapers had carried full-page advertisements announcing the opening of Delgado Diamonds' flagship store in Bond Street, and Cruz had been a guest on a morning television programme, speaking about the lavish party he would be hosting that evening to celebrate the launch.

The flirtatious female interviewer had clearly been smitten by Cruz's charisma, Sabrina remembered irritably. Many women would leap at the chance of an affair with a millionaire diamond tycoon, but she refused to sacrifice her self-respect by becoming his mistress, even to save Eversleigh Hall. *But what of her brother's hopes of training to be a pilot?* her conscience questioned. Could she, *should* she agree to Cruz's demands for Tristan's sake?

The sound of her phone pulled her from her thoughts, and she answered a call from the horse dealer who explained that he had found a buyer for Monty. Her heart plummeted at the news, even though she desperately needed the money from the sale.

If she sold herself to Cruz, she would not need to sell her horse, whispered the voice in her head.

But although Cruz had offered to pay her over a million pounds, the sum would only cover the renovation work after the fire and leave her with enough money to maintain the estate until Earl Bancroft returned or was declared dead. Sabrina knew she would still have to live to a tight budget, which would not include the up-keep of a horse. It was a bitter irony that if she sold Eversleigh to the hotel chain she would be able to afford Monty, but she would not have anywhere to keep him and she would not have a home herself. While her future was so uncertain, it seemed kinder to sell Monty to a new owner who could give him a secure home.

Her mind was in turmoil and she gave up trying to work on the cabinet and went to get changed into her riding clothes. Monty greeted her with the snuffling noise he always made when he saw her, and when Sabrina led him out of his stable he nuzzled his nose against her shoulder. Hopefully it would not take him long to get used to his new owner, she thought bleakly. Monty whinnied with delight when she led him into the jumping ring. He loved to jump, and Sabrina was determined to enjoy her last precious ride on him.

'Come on, boy,' she whispered in his ear as they approached the first fence. She held her breath as she felt the power and strength of the horse beneath her, and then the two of them were flying through the air as Monty cleared the fence with inches to spare.

As Cruz climbed out of his car he noted that the bright red Ferrari looked gaudy and out of place parked on the driveway in front of

Eversleigh Hall. A Rolls-Royce or a Bentley would suit the elegant grandeur of the stately home far better than a brash sports car. He grimaced as he once again recalled the comment he'd overheard Lord Porchester make about him being one of the *nouveau riche*. Porchester hadn't minded borrowing money from him, Cruz thought sardonically. And if Sabrina had any sense she would accept his offer of financial assistance that would enable her to keep her family's home.

He'd caught sight of her riding her horse as he drove along the lane leading to the Eversleigh estate, and instead of walking up to the front door he made his way around the side of the house, heading towards the stables.

She was a superb horsewoman, Cruz acknowledged as he leaned against the paddock fence and admired Sabrina's skill and perfect timing as horse and rider sailed over a six-foot wall made out of polystyrene bricks.

'That was impressive,' he commented when she rode up to him and dismounted. She was wearing her riding gear again. When she bent over to pick up the horse's reins, Cruz watched the stretchy material of her jodhpurs tighten across her pert derrière and felt his body tighten in response.

Santa mãe! How could he want her so badly? What spell had she cast on him that had decimated his ability to think of anything but her and his consuming longing to feel her soft body beneath him?

She unfastened the strap beneath her chin and as she lifted off her riding helmet her blonde hair cascaded down her back like a river of silk. Cruz almost groaned out loud. When they had been together he had loved her hair, loved the way it felt against his skin when she had straddled him and leaned forwards so that the long golden strands brushed his chest.

His jaw clenched. Once he had loved her, and for a while he had even managed to kid himself that she was in love with him. What a fool he had been to think that a woman of Sabrina's class and refinement would give up her life of privilege and luxury for a poorly paid, poorly educated miner.

'Why are you here?' Her cultured voice pulled Cruz from the past. 'You told me I had until seven o'clock this evening to give you my answer.'

Sabrina led Monty back to the stables and was supremely conscious of Cruz walking beside her. She despised the way her heart had missed a beat when she'd noticed him watching her ride. In black trousers and shirt, his eyes hidden behind designer shades, he was devastatingly handsome and a dangerous threat to her peace of mind.

Katie, the teenage groom, was waiting in the yard and took Monty into his stall to unsaddle him.

'Do you only keep one horse here?' Cruz glanced at the five empty stables.

Sabrina nodded. 'When I was a child all the stables were occupied. My mother had a couple of hunters and a horse for dressage, and my brother and I learned to ride on ponies.' Her voice faltered. 'Soon there will be no horses at Eversleigh. Monty is to be sold.'

'Tears, *gatinha*?' Cruz caught hold of her chin

to prevent her from turning away and captured the sparkle of moisture clinging to her lashes with his thumb pad. He noted the dark shadows beneath her eyes that looked like bruises on her porcelain skin. Her lower lip quivered almost imperceptibly before she firmed it and her air of vulnerability made his gut twist.

Abruptly he released her and thrust his hands into his pockets. 'You can cry over a horse, yet you did not cry when you lost our child,' he said harshly. 'But I know you regretted your pregnancy and perhaps you did not find the loss of our baby so terrible.'

Sabrina stared at his hard face and the arrogant line of his mouth and a fierce rage simmered inside her. 'Not terrible?' she choked. 'The day of the miscarriage was the worst day of my life. I was utterly heartbroken when I lost Luiz.' At Cruz's look of surprise, she went on to explain, 'We'd discussed baby names. When I was miscarrying they scanned me at the hospital and could see that we were expecting a boy. Although he never lived in the world, he lived inside me for seventeen weeks and I wanted him to have a name.'

She felt a couple of spots of rain and glanced up to see ominous dark clouds had covered the sun. But she ignored the imminent storm as the storm inside her became an unstoppable force. 'How can you suggest that I wasn't affected by the miscarriage? I was devastated.'

'If you were, you hid it well.' Cruz's tone seemed to imply that he did not believe her. 'You did not appear grief-stricken—and I should know. After I was born my parents tried unsuccessfully for many years to have another child. My mother suffered several miscarriages and each time she lost a baby she was beside herself with grief. My overriding memory of my childhood was hearing my mother sobbing,' he said grimly.

'After a few months she would be happy because she was pregnant again, but each of her pregnancies ended in more tears and heartache and there was nothing that I or my father could do to comfort her. My mother believed it was a miracle when she eventually gave birth to my twin sisters, fourteen years after she'd had me.'

Sabrina stared at him. Ten years ago he had not spoken about what had happened to his mother, and his revelation now gave a new insight to why he had been overly protective during her pregnancy. 'I appreciate that your mother must have been distraught every time she suffered a miscarriage. Everyone deals with things differently and at the time we lost Luiz I was in a state of shock and I couldn't cry. But that wasn't because I didn't care.' She was shaking with anger now. 'How dare you judge me because my reaction to losing my baby was different from your mother's? And how dare you say that I had regretted falling pregnant? If you believe that, it proves that you never really knew me, and you certainly didn't care about me. All you wanted was our child.'

Her voice rose as her words spilled out in a furious torrent. 'Nothing has changed. You didn't want me then and you don't want me now. The only reason you're willing to pay me to be your mistress is for my social skills and because you think my connections with the aristocracy will boost sales for your jewellery company. Well, I am not for sale!'

She whirled away from him and ran across the yard, heading towards the nearest shelter from the rain that was now falling hard. By the time she reached the hay shed her jacket was soaked and she wrenched open the buttons and tugged her arms out of the sleeves.

'*I don't want you?* That's a laugh,' Cruz's voice growled close to her ear.

Sabrina spun round and gasped as he snaked his arm around her waist and hauled her against his muscular and very aroused body. She looked up at his face and saw no evidence of laughter on his hard-boned features, only a savage determination that made her heart lurch.

'Does this feel like I do not want you, *gatinha*?' he demanded. He gave her no chance to reply as he captured her mouth with his and kissed her with a fierce hunger, crushing her lips as he sought to crush her resistance with his urgent desire.

CHAPTER SEVEN

He filled her senses, and beneath his hands her body became alive, every skin cell and nerve-ending quivering with pleasure at his touch. But Sabrina still felt blazingly angry at how badly he had misjudged her at the time of the miscarriage. When she was eighteen she had put Cruz on a pedestal and thought he could do no wrong. But now she was older and wiser and she knew he was a mortal man with strengths but also weaknesses.

She was determined not to be overwhelmed by him as she had been in the past. His physical strength was superior to hers, but she was not going to submissively let him have things all his own way. His mouth was creating havoc as he trailed his lips over her cheek to her ear and his sharp teeth bit her tender lobe. She repressed a shudder of longing and renewed her attempts to resist him, but her wild struggling had a counter-effect, she discovered, as she felt his rock-hard arousal push against her thigh.

His arms were like bands of steel around her, making escape impossible. He slid one hand down and splayed his fingers over her buttocks, urging her into even closer contact with the solid ridge of his manhood straining beneath his trousers. Sabrina gasped as he circled his hips against her pelvis, and in a corner of her mind she registered that he could not be faking his desire. Cruz was on fire for her and she was melting in his heat.

His other hand tangled in her hair as he angled her head and kissed her mouth again, forcing her lips apart so that his tongue could plunder her inner sweetness. He kissed her as if he could not have enough of her, as if he had fought a battle with himself and lost.

'I wish I did not want you,' he muttered when he finally wrenched his mouth from hers to allow them both to drag oxygen into their lungs. 'You are like a drug in my veins, so bloody addictive that I can't resist you even though I know I should for the sake of my sanity.'

His words made no sense to Sabrina. How could she be a threat to Cruz's sanity? It was the other way round, and it was imperative that she found the strength of will to resist him. He still had one hand clamped on her bottom, and he moved his other hand to the front of her shirt. Her heart gave a jolt when he began to unfasten the buttons, but she did not stop him, couldn't, if she was brutally honest.

Excitement spiralled inside her as he pushed her shirt off her shoulders to reveal her plain white bra. She wished she were wearing sexy underwear in black satin and lace, but then Cruz traced his fingers over the outline of her nipple visible through the stretchy material of her bra and she caught her breath as a shaft of exquisite pleasure shot through her.

'It doesn't help that you are so damned responsive,' he said harshly. He reached around her back to unfasten her bra and tugged the straps down her arms, baring her breasts to his hot gaze. His voice thickened. 'How the hell am

I supposed to resist you when your body tells me that you are as hungry as I am?'

Sabrina shivered when he cupped her naked breasts in his hands, but it was not cold that made her nipples harden into burgeoning points but anticipation and uncontrollable sexual excitement. Cruz gave a husky laugh as he flicked his thumb pads across her nipples and heard her swiftly indrawn breath.

'I remember you used to love it when I caressed your breasts with my hands and especially my mouth. Do you still like that, *gatinha*?' He gave another low chuckle when he realised that she was incapable of replying. 'Let's find out, shall we?'

Dimly she knew she should stop him and bring an end to this madness, but she was enraptured by the feel of his warm hands on her flesh, seduced by his soft words of promise. He lifted her into his arms and laid her down on the pile of square hay bales. The hay felt scratchy beneath her shoulders but she forgot the slight discomfort as Cruz knelt over her and lowered his head to her breast. He drew her nipple into his mouth and suckled her hard. The pleasure was so intense that she gave a keening cry and curled her fingers into his shoulders to urge him to continue his exquisite torment.

He needed no persuading, pausing only to transfer his mouth to her other nipple. 'Oh, God!' she groaned as deep shudders of pleasure racked her body when he flicked his tongue back and forth over the tender peak. She could feel the fire building low in her pelvis as he continued his merciless ravishment of her body. Reality faded and she was aware only of the sweet smell of hay, the sound of the rain drumming on the roof of the shed and Cruz's uneven breaths as he took his mouth from her breast and claimed her lips in a deep, drugging kiss that ravaged her soul.

This was the Cruz she remembered from the past. He might wear expensive clothes now, instead of jeans, and drink champagne rather than beer, but the essence of him hadn't changed and her senses recognised the familiar musk of male pheromones and the subtle scent that was uniquely him.

She ran her hands over his soaking-wet shirt and tugged open the buttons before pushing the material over his shoulders. His bronzed chest was satin overlaid with black hairs that felt like silk beneath her fingertips as she traced the ridges of his powerful pectoral and abdominal muscles.

He was so beautiful. And so massively aroused! Desire flooded through her when he bore his weight down on her so that her breasts were crushed against his bare chest and she was supremely conscious of his erection pressing into the junction between her thighs. Their clothes were an unwanted barrier. The fire inside her burned hotter and became an inferno of feverish need, and she sensed from the fierce intensity of Cruz's kiss that he had passed the point of no return.

He tugged the zip of her jodhpurs down but struggled to pull the clingy trousers over her hips.

'These were not designed for easy access,' he growled impatiently.

The sound of his voice broke through the sexual haze surrounding Sabrina's brain and forced her to acknowledge a vital fact.

'I'm not on the pill,' she muttered.

Cruz did not seem to hear her as he managed to slip his hand inside her jodhpurs and stroked a finger over the damp panel of her knickers. Instinctively she arched her hips and a shudder of longing ran through her when he eased the panel aside and touched her eager flesh. But her common sense could not be ignored. She would never risk another unplanned pregnancy and she pulled at his hand to make him stop his intimate exploration.

'We can't. I'm not protected.'

This time he heard and he lifted his head and stared down at her, his eyes glittering with frustration before he swore savagely and rolled away. He lay on his back on the hay bales and held his forearm across his eyes—almost, Sabrina thought, as if he was ashamed of what emotions they might reveal. But he could not disguise the ragged sound of his breathing or the heaving of his chest as he dragged air into his lungs. Outside, the rain fell harder and somehow the thunderous drumming on the roof and the feeling that they were trapped in the hay shed made the prickling atmosphere even tenser.

'Cruz…' She flinched as he leapt to his feet and could not disguise her shock when she saw his tortured expression.

He gave a bitter laugh. 'So now you have discovered the truth. How does it feel to know that you have the power to bring a grown man to his knees? *Of course I damn well want you.*' He threw the words at her as if the confession had been ripped from his soul. 'I wanted you ten years ago and nothing has changed. I desire you more than I have ever desired any other woman. You are my nemesis, *gatinha.*' His lip curled in self-mockery. 'No doubt you are gloating at my weakness?'

'No,' she said shakily. His self-contempt touched something inside her and she stretched her hand towards him. 'Cruz, I…'

He swore again and snatched up his shirt, thrusting his arms into the sleeves with such violent force that the material ripped. *Deus*, was that pity he had heard in Sabrina's voice? Cruz felt humiliated by his inability to resist her and his anger made him want to verbally lash out at her.

'However much you might wish to deny it, you want me as badly as I want you. We are both gripped by this madness, and neither of us will know any peace until we have sated our desire for each other.'

He strode over to the door and turned to look at her, his mouth curling into a mocking smile as he noted her flushed face and rumpled hair before he dropped his gaze deliberately to her breasts. 'Your body betrays you,' he drawled, and laughed softly when she grabbed her shirt and held it in front of her to hide her swollen, reddened nipples.

'You have two hours left before your deadline expires and you lose your only chance to safeguard your home. Think of the benefits. As my mistress you will enjoy six months of the best sex you've ever known. I don't believe any other man has turned you on as much as I do,' he taunted.

'Go to hell!' Infuriated beyond endurance, Sabrina grabbed an old horseshoe that was lying on the floor and flung it at Cruz. But he had already walked out of the door and the iron shoe clattered on the flagstones of the stable yard.

She watched him stride across the yard until he had disappeared from view and then flopped down on the hay bales, breathing hard as if she had run a marathon. No one but Cruz Delgado had ever made her feel so furiously angry. And he had been right, damn him—so turned on!

Her hands were shaking too much to be able to fasten her bra and she gave up and pulled on her shirt, wincing as the material scraped over her acutely sensitive nipples. The ache of unfulfilled sexual desire slowly ebbed from her body but the image of Cruz's tormented expression lingered in her mind.

It was not true that he had only asked her to be his mistress because her aristocratic background would be useful to his business.

Cruz wanted her in his bed and he had actually admitted that he desired her more than any other woman. The realisation that he wanted her for herself above any other reason gave her a feeling of liberation and her self-confidence soared.

During her childhood, and especially her teenage years, she had felt rejected by both her parents and the feeling that she was somehow not good enough had made her anxious to please people. She had striven to be a perfect daughter and a perfect sister to her younger brother, even though it had often meant sublimating her hopes and desires out of a sense of duty to her family.

Rarely had she put herself first or thought about what she wanted, Sabrina realised. But Cruz's admission freed her from her insecurities and she acknowledged that what she wanted and desired more than anything was *him.*

He had stated that neither of them would have any peace until they had sated their desire for each other, and she could not deny it was the truth. She had never forgotten him and she recognised that subconsciously she had compared every man she'd dated to Cruz. *Dear God!* After ten years he was still in her system, she thought with a flash of despair. She had allowed herself to be held back by the past for far too long. But if she agreed to be his mistress in a sex-without-strings affair she hoped she could walk away from him at the end of six months, having gained closure, and finally be able to move forwards with her life.

The vintage champagne cost eight hundred pounds a bottle and the caviar was Iranian beluga. Only the absolute finest—and most expensive, Cruz thought sardonically—delicacies were good enough to be served to the exclusive guests attending the exclusive party to celebrate the launch of Delgado Diamonds' new premises in Bond Street.

The flagship store was spread over four floors and had been designed in a contemporary and ultra-luxurious style. The party was taking place in the main salon where the lacquered walnut-panelled walls and Italian marble floors provided a stunning backdrop for exquisite crystal chandeliers suspended from the double-height ceiling, which gave the room a feeling of lofty grandeur.

Cruz sipped his champagne and looked around the room at the guests who were milling between glass display cabinets admiring jewellery presented on black velvet cushions. Discreet lighting added to the ambiance of the room, and the soft hum of muted conversation was barely disturbed by the faint clink of glasses borne on silver trays by the waiters.

He had come a long way from the *favela* in Belo Horizonte, and the mine at Montes Claros. He wondered what his guests would think of him if he revealed that once he had spent his days underground digging diamonds out of rock. Few people knew the truth of his background and he preferred to keep it that way. He was not ashamed of the fact that he had clawed his way out of poverty, but he was finding it hard enough to be accepted into high society, and it was better that he was regarded as a man of mystery than a beggar from the gutter, he thought cynically.

He pictured Sabrina when she had visited his

Kensington apartment looking the epitome of elegance in a black cocktail dress and pearls. In his head he heard her cool voice crisply informing him that she would not demean herself to have sex with him. She had forgotten her high ideals when he had kissed her at the stables earlier today. His body tightened involuntarily as he remembered her soft moans of pleasure when he had flicked his tongue across her turgid nipples. When he had tumbled her down in the hay she had lost her airs and graces and turned into the sensual wildcat she had been in Brazil.

He shifted his position in an effort to ease the nagging ache in his groin and cursed his impatience that had made him come on to her with an embarrassing lack of finesse instead of his usual laid-back charm. *Why was he even bothering to pursue her?* he asked himself. At least half the women at the party were sending him signals that they were available and he knew he could have any one of them in his bed with minimum effort on his part. But the only woman he wanted was not here and he could only look forward to another night of sexual frustration.

A ripple of activity over by the door caught his attention and he assumed a guest had arrived late to the party. He could not see past the burly bodyguard, but inexplicably he felt the hairs on the back of his neck prickle.

For some reason, the proverb ‘clothes maketh the man’ slipped into Sabrina’s mind, but it was a new dress that was making this particular woman feel slightly more confident—and at this moment she needed all the self-confidence she could get!

Strictly speaking, the midnight-blue silk crepe gown with narrow diamanté shoulder straps wasn’t new. She had bought it last year when she had still been able to afford to buy haute couture but had never had the opportunity to wear it until now. As she entered the main salon of Delgado Diamonds’ opulent Mayfair store she breathed a sigh of relief that her name had been on the guest list and she had avoided an argument with the security guard, or, even worse, the humiliation of being escorted from the premises.

Although that could happen if Cruz had decided to withdraw his offer of financial assistance for Eversleigh Hall in return for her agreement to be his mistress. The gold clock on the wall told her that it was an hour past the deadline of seven p.m. that Cruz had given her.

He was standing at the far end of the salon and the enigmatic expression on his chiselled features gave no clue to his thoughts. Taking a deep breath, Sabrina sauntered towards him, but her heart was thudding in her chest and she fought an urge to run back out to the street away from Cruz's cynical gaze and the curious glances from the other party guests.

She forced herself to keep walking forwards, conscious that the click of her stiletto heels on the marble floor sounded overly loud in the silence that had settled over the room. Her eyes darted to either side of her and she recognised several arts correspondents from national newspapers who were presumably here to report on the party. If Cruz publicly rejected her the whole country would be able to read about it.

Instead of dwelling on that potentially embarrassing scenario she focused on him. He was devastating in a formal black dinner suit and a snow-white shirt that contrasted with his darkly tanned face and throat. She halted in front of him and forgot every word of the speech she had rehearsed on the way here.

Cruz's eyes were hooded as if he wished to hide his thoughts from her, but the rigid set of his jaw betrayed his tension. Sabrina felt the fierce pull of attraction between them and exhilaration swept through her. Words were unnecessary, she decided as she stepped closer to him, so close that their hips touched and her body burned in his heat.

Despite her three-inch heels she had to go up on tiptoe to wind her arms around his neck and pull his head down level with hers. She felt his shoulder muscles clench as she covered his mouth with hers and kissed him.

At first he did not respond and she felt a rising sense of panic as she acknowledged that she was going to look very foolish if he pushed her away and called the security guards to escort her from the building. In desperation she nipped his lower lip with her teeth and a violent shudder ran through him. She was startled, her lashes flew open and she saw a feral hunger in his eyes as he took control and stole her breath with a kiss that plundered her soul.

He kissed her fiercely, feverishly, as if for the past ten years he had missed her as much as she had missed him. He roamed his hands up and down her spine, seemingly unconcerned by the fact that they were making a very public spectacle, and as Sabrina sank deeper into the velvet darkness of desire she lost all awareness of her surroundings and there was only Cruz.

When at last he lifted his mouth from hers she swayed on her feet and stared at him dazedly, unaware of the storm of emotions that darkened her eyes to the colour of wet slate.

'You're late,' he drawled. Sabrina knew he was not referring to her late arrival at the party. How could he sound so cool and seem so unaffected? she wondered as she soothed her ravaged lips with the tip of her tongue. It would be easy to feel overawed by him as she had been ten years ago, but she was no longer an innocent girl and her mouth curved into a sensual smile.

'But worth waiting for,' she murmured.

'I'll hold you to that promise later tonight.' He spoke softly so that the journalists who had crowded around them did not hear him, but Sabrina heard the warning in his words and for a moment her nerve nearly failed her as she faced up to the fact that she had sold her body and possibly her soul to a man who ten years ago had stolen her heart.

Triumph surged through Cruz as he ran his eyes over Sabrina. She looked stunning and desire flooded hot and fierce through his veins. The launch party of Delgado Diamonds represented the pinnacle of his success, but he felt frustrated knowing that it would be several hours before he would be free from his responsibilities and could take her to bed.

He liked the fact that she had developed from

a shy teenager who had been a virgin when they'd met ten years ago into a sexually confident woman with the self-assurance to come on to him. But when he studied her closely he saw a vulnerable expression in her eyes and noticed the almost imperceptible tremor of her lower lip that caused him to feel a faint pang of regret.

Ten years ago she had broken his heart, and with a sudden, uncomfortable flash of insight he recognised that he had given her the ultimatum because he wanted to punish her for leaving him. What kind of man planned to use sex as a means of retribution? he asked himself with self-contempt. The past no longer mattered. He felt no emotional connection to Sabrina now, and he would never again confuse lust with love. His attraction to her was purely sexual, as he assumed hers was to him. There was no reason why they should not enjoy a physical relationship and in six months he would walk away from her, his sexual hunger sated, and hopefully with the map in his possession. He was jerked from his introspection when one of the journalists spoke.

'Lady Sabrina, can you confirm that you are in a relationship with Mr Delgado?'

Sabrina tore her eyes from Cruz, wishing she knew what he was thinking behind his shuttered expression. She glanced at the reporter. 'I thought I just did,' she said drily.

It was inevitable that pictures of them locked in a passionate kiss would feature in many of tomorrow's papers. There was a ripple of laughter and she became aware of her surroundings once more: guests dressed in formal evening clothes, white-jacketed waiters serving canapés on silver platters, a buzz of conversation as the party resumed.

She had attended countless such events and felt on familiar ground as Cruz guided her around the room and introduced her to the other guests. She was acquainted with many of them. Cruz was right to think that the English aristocracy was a tightly knit group, partly because historically marriages between the landed gentry had been encouraged. At least two of the guests were Sabrina's distant cousins.

She found herself relaxing as she sipped

champagne and chatted about a new art gallery that had opened in Chelsea and the excellent production of *La Traviata* at the Royal Opera House. Cruz revealed a broad knowledge of the arts and current affairs and Sabrina noted that he cleverly steered every topic of conversation around to his jewellery company.

She was continually aware of his presence by her side, of his hand placed lightly in the small of her back that seemed to burn through her dress and scorch her skin. As the evening drew to an end and the guests started to leave the party her tension grew, and on the short drive to Kensington in Cruz's chauffeur-driven limousine her silence earned a comment from him.

'You're very quiet suddenly.'

She chewed her lip. 'I suppose you are wondering why I changed my mind about…' She struggled to continue as the reality that she had agreed to have sex with him for one and a half million pounds sank into her brain.

'About selling yourself to me,' Cruz drawled. He shrugged. 'It's not a mystery. I knew you would do anything to save your beloved Eversleigh Hall—' his tone hardened '—even if it means having to demean yourself by sleeping with me.'

'I'll pay you back the money as soon as my father returns. And if he doesn't…' her voice faltered '…if he is declared dead I will be given access to his bank accounts and I'll be able to reimburse you out of my inheritance.'

She stared at the angles of Cruz's sculpted profile illuminated by the street lamps and felt as though she were looking at a stranger. 'Saving Eversleigh wasn't my only reason,' she said huskily. 'Meeting you again has made me realise that there are unresolved issues between us from ten years ago. There are things we need to talk about, in particular how we both felt after I miscarried our baby…' she hesitated '…and how we feel about each other now.'

'I've told you how I feel.' Cruz sounded bored of the conversation. 'I want to have sex with you and I am prepared to pay for the privilege of having you as my mistress for the next six months.' His glittering gaze pierced the shadowy darkness of the interior of the car and raked across Sabrina's pale face. 'We made a business deal,' he reminded her. 'What happened between us in the past is irrelevant.'

'What about the future?' she asked in a low voice.

He frowned. 'If you are asking me if we might have a future, then my answer is a categorical no. I'm not looking for a long-term relationship with you or anyone else.'

Until two minutes ago Sabrina's thoughts had been focused on the night ahead. She hadn't cared about the future—at least that was what she had convinced herself. But Cruz's unequivocal statement that he would not want a relationship with her beyond her six-month stint as his mistress was unexpectedly hurtful. Of course there was no possibility that she would fall in love with him, she told herself firmly. She had been there, done that and her heart bore the scars.

The car pulled into the underground car park, and as Cruz ushered her into the lift she felt a rising sense of panic that maybe she was making the biggest mistake of her life. She debated telling him that she had changed her mind and could not go through with their *business deal.*

She had to do whatever it took to safeguard Eversleigh for future generations of the Bancroft family, whispered the voice of her conscience. And her brother's future career as a pilot was dependent on her being able to raise the aviation school's fees.

While the lift made its smooth ascent to the top floor she could not tear her eyes from Cruz. He had undone his bow tie and the top few buttons of his shirt and she could see a sprinkling of black hairs that she knew covered his chest and arrowed down over his flat stomach. Her mouth felt suddenly dry as she pictured the fuzz of body hair running below the waistband of his trousers and becoming thicker around the base of his manhood.

The light-headed feeling she was experiencing had nothing to do with the one glass of champagne she'd had at the party, she acknowledged ruefully. Her body felt as though she were on fire and the core of her need was centred low in her pelvis. She tried convincing herself that the reason she was so intensely turned on was because she hadn't had sex for two years—and that one occasion, with a guy she had dated for a few months, had been unfulfilling. But as her eyes moved back up Cruz's lean, hard body and connected with his sultry gaze she knew she was kidding herself.

She wanted him more than she had ever wanted anyone or anything in her life.

She had not come to him for the sake of Eversleigh or her brother's career or from a sense of duty to protect her family's long history. For the first time in her life she was choosing to put her needs first and the sense of freedom she felt was wildly exhilarating.

Cruz's sexy mouth promised heaven and she instinctively moistened her lips with the tip of her tongue as she imagined him kissing her. The lift halted and the doors opened directly into his penthouse apartment.

'If you've changed your mind, say so now,' he advised.

Her heart was thudding unevenly, but she said steadily, 'I haven't changed my mind.'

To her surprise she saw dull colour flare along his cheekbones, and she suddenly realised that he wasn't as in control as he wanted her to think.

'Then come here.'

She went unhesitatingly, and he swept her up into his arms and strode purposefully down the hallway of the apartment into the master bedroom.

CHAPTER EIGHT

HE KNEW WHY Sabrina was here, Cruz reminded himself. She would do anything to safeguard her family's ancestral home and as she couldn't sell him the Estrela Vermelha she was prepared to sell him her body. He felt an unexpected flicker of regret that he'd had to coerce her into being his mistress, but his common sense told him it was better to have a business arrangement that negated the risk of emotions becoming involved.

In the car she had said that she wanted them to talk about their past relationship. Why did women always want to discuss their emotions and everyone else's? he thought irritably. Sabrina had not been interested in his emotions ten years ago. She had rushed back to England and left him alone to grieve for their baby, and she hadn't spared him a second thought.

Talking was definitely not on his agenda, Cruz decided. Mindless sex without emotional baggage was a far better option, which would allow him to stay in control. A control that was already being tested, he realised, aware that he was harder than he could ever remember being as he set Sabrina on her feet and her breasts brushed against his chest. He had planned on a slow, skilful seduction intended to drive her to the brink so that she begged for his possession.

His pride still stung when he remembered her telling him that she would not demean herself by having sex with him. He wanted to show her that she was just another blonde in his bed. But he had never felt this hungry for any other woman, he acknowledged grimly.

His heart had given a peculiar lurch when she'd arrived at the party dressed to kill in a gown that looked as if she had been poured into it and with her hair flowing like a river of pale gold silk down her back. All evening he'd felt an ache of anticipation in his gut. But now that the moment was here, *Deus*, he felt like a teenager on a first date. He wanted to please her, he wanted sex to be perfect for her—he wanted to show her what she had been missing all these years since she left him.

The subtle fragrance of her perfume teased his senses and he felt an almost painful tug of desire in his groin. He needed to take control before he succumbed to his primitive instincts and took her hard and fast as his body was clamouring to do.

Her lips were slightly parted as if she was expecting him to kiss her, as if she wanted him to. He resisted and walked over to the bed, quickly stripping down to his underwear before he stretched out on top of the satin bedspread and propped himself up on one elbow.

'You look very beautiful in that dress, but I want to see you naked. Take it off,' he commanded.

Sabrina's stomach muscles clenched as she stared at Cruz's handsome face and then dropped her gaze to his bare chest covered in whorls of dark hairs. Her attention was drawn lower to the very obvious bulge beneath his boxer shorts. He was gorgeous! She could not take her eyes from the outline of his massive arousal and she felt a flicker of doubt, knowing she'd not had sex for a long time. She hoped he would take things slowly, but the molten sensation between her thighs was proof that her body was way ahead of her and was already preparing to accommodate him.

She wished he'd held her in his arms and undressed her, but he was paying her a lot of money to please him, she thought ruefully as she reached behind her to unzip her dress and drew the shoulder straps down her arms. The dark blue silk pooled at her feet and her body burned as Cruz ran his eyes over her sheer black lace strapless bra and matching knickers.

'Very pretty,' he murmured. 'Did you choose your sexy underwear for me, *gatinha*?'

She thought of denying it, but what would be the point? Her mind flew back to a few hours earlier when she had made her preparations to become Cruz's mistress. After soaking in a bath scented with fragrant oil, she had smoothed moisturiser onto every inch of her skin before dressing in exquisite lingerie.

'Of course,' she told him in a husky voice that she barely recognised as her own.

The sound of his swiftly indrawn breath made her feel powerful in a way that she had never experienced before. Tonight she wasn't Sabrina the serious historian, or Sabrina the dutiful daughter. She was a temptress, desired above all other women by the sexiest man on the planet.

'I always sleep naked, and while you are my mistress I expect you to do the same,' Cruz drawled. 'Take your bra off.'

She sensed a power struggle between them and rebellion flared inside her as she looked at him sprawled on the bed like a sultan who had commanded his favourite concubine to pleasure him. But there was no escaping the truth that she had sold herself to him. Pride whipped her head up. If he wanted a whore he would damn well get one!

She deliberately held his gaze as once again she reached behind her and unfastened her bra.

The cups fell away to reveal her firm breasts adorned with dusky pink tips.

'Very pretty,' he repeated, but this time his voice was husky with need and his Brazilian accent was as sensual as molten chocolate. 'We made an arrangement, Sabrina, and earlier tonight one and a half million pounds was transferred into your bank account. Now it's your turn to fulfil your side of the deal.'

She wondered if he was deliberately trying to make her feel like a tramp. But she discovered that she did not care. She wanted him so badly that her body throbbed with a deep drumbeat that pulsed insistently between her legs, and her desire intensified when he slipped off his boxers and revealed the swollen length of his manhood. The sight of his potent virility made her feel weak with longing.

Cruz settled himself comfortably against the pillows and folded his arms behind his head. He trailed his eyes over Sabrina's delectable body. Her lace knickers were provocative rather than practical and barely covered the triangle of downy blonde hair at the top of her thighs.

'I want to see *all* of you,' he ordered.

Sabrina felt no embarrassment as she stripped for him. The feral glitter in his eyes made her feel intensely desirable and she hooked her fingers in the top of her panties and pulled them slowly down her legs, revealing herself to him inch by inch and almost purring with feline pleasure when he gave an audible groan. She knew she looked good. Her body was toned, with a slender waist and full, rounded breasts that jutted proudly forwards.

Her eyes didn't leave his as she sauntered round to the empty side of the bed. A spark of rebelliousness prompted her to ask coolly, 'Is there a particular position you want me to adopt?'

'Don't push your luck, *gatinha.*' Cruz watched her lie down beside him. 'You look like a vestal virgin preparing to offer yourself up for sacrifice,' he mocked. 'We can start with the missionary position by all means. But you will have to open your legs—or I'll do it for you,' he warned softly when she did not move.

'Cruz…' She choked out his name, appalled

that it seemed he really did intend to take her body without finesse, but she was even more appalled by the searing lust that swept through her at the prospect of surrendering herself so utterly to his possession.

Casting a fulminating look at his hard-boned face, she spread her legs a little.

'Wider.'

She hesitated fractionally before obeying him. With her legs now open in a vee shape she felt exposed and she smelled the sweet musk of her arousal and knew Cruz could smell it too. Her heart was beating unevenly, but deep down a part of her revelled in his masterful commands. She didn't want to think, or question her decision to sell herself to him. She was tired of responsibility and duty and always trying to do the right thing for other people and she wanted Cruz to take charge and give her hot, hard sex.

She wished he would roll on top of her and penetrate her with his powerful erection. She wanted him to touch her intimately and probe her with his fingers, and she instinctively arched her hips in mute supplication.

He laughed softly. 'Patience, *gatinha*. Anticipation is part of the pleasure, don't you think?' She made an inarticulate sound and he laughed again and unfolded her hands from her breasts before he bent his head and lazily flicked his tongue across one pink nipple so that it swelled and tightened. He repeated the action to her other nipple and drew the hard tip into his mouth, eliciting a husky moan from her.

Triumph surged through Cruz. Sabrina's response was exactly what he intended. His jaw hardened. She might find having sex with him demeaning, but she wanted him all the same.

He continued to play with her nipples, suckling each in turn while at the same time rolling the other between his fingers and eliciting helpless little whimpers from her. Oh, yes, she wanted him. He lifted his head and looked down at her flushed face. Her eyes were wide, her pupils dilated as she silently implored him.

It pleased him that she was so desperate. From the moment he had seen Sabrina again at Eversleigh Hall he had planned his revenge, and discovering that she had financial problems had given him the leverage to force her into his bed. Cruz suddenly felt sickened by himself. What the hell had he been thinking? He would never force a woman to do anything against her will. But he was not forcing Sabrina, he reminded himself. She was here of her own free choice and she had made it clear that she was prepared to have sex with him to safeguard her home.

'Cruz.' She murmured his name like a prayer, and the pleading note in her voice touched something deep inside him.

'Is this what you want, *querida*?' he whispered against her lips as he trailed his hand over her stomach and thighs that were parted for him, and slid a finger into her silken folds.

Her reaction was instant. She jerked her hips upwards, offering her body to him and giving a guttural cry as he pushed deeper inside her.

'Yes…*oh*…yes.'

Sabrina almost came when Cruz finally touched her where she desperately wanted him to. She was so wet for him that foreplay was unnecessary. She wanted him inside her now, *now*…

She gave a sob of frustration when he withdrew his finger but her momentary panic that he was enjoying teasing her faded as she watched him rip open a condom packet and deftly sheath himself. His eyes glittered with purpose and something else she could not define. Cruz wanted emotionless sex, she reminded herself. So it could not have been regret that she'd glimpsed in his olive-green depths. It must have been the shadow cast by the bedside lamp. Her thoughts scattered as he leaned over her and kissed her mouth passionately but with an unexpected tenderness that completely unravelled her.

He was Cruz, her Cruz, and she had missed him so much. With a soft sigh she stroked his cheek and moved her hand up to run her fingers through his springy black hair while he took the kiss even deeper, drugging her senses with his sensual exploration of her lips.

He kept his mouth on hers as he positioned himself over her, and she instinctively bent her knees as he pressed forwards and entered her with a powerful thrust that drove the breath from her lungs. He felt the slight resistance of her body and paused, his voice thick with remorse as he muttered, 'Did I hurt you?'

'No.' Sabrina forced herself to relax, allowing her internal muscles to stretch around him. 'It's been a while since I last did this,' she admitted with faint embarrassment in her voice. Feeling him begin to withdraw, she clutched his shoulders and urged him down onto her. 'Don't stop.'

Cruz had no intention of stopping. Sabrina's confession that there had been no other man in her life recently had decimated the last vestiges of his restraint, and he groaned and thrust into her again, driven by an intensity of need that shocked him because it was utterly beyond his control. It was just sex, he reminded himself. Very, very good sex—but he had known it would be. The sexual connection he felt with Sabrina went beyond anything he'd felt for any other woman. He set a rhythm that she quickly matched, and with deep, measured strokes he reclaimed her and possessed her utterly.

He felt the first ripples of her orgasm and heard her gasp as the spasms grew stronger and her muscles clenched around him, inciting him to increase his pace as he drove them both higher. Cruz's sole aim was to ensure her pleasure, and he tormented her nipples with his tongue, lapping each swollen peak in turn until she suddenly gave a cry and arched like a bow beneath him.

For a few seconds he held her at the edge, testing the limits of his self-control, and then drove into her again, deeper and harder, and felt the explosion of her climax. She wrapped her legs around his back and her fingers gripped his buttocks. The sensation of her fingernails raking across his flesh was beyond his endurance. Pleasure surged through him in an unstoppable force, causing him to lose control spectacularly. Eyes closed, his head thrown back so that the cords in his neck strained, his groan was wrenched from his soul as his body shuddered with the exquisite ecstasy of sexual release.

For a long time afterwards neither of them moved. Sabrina felt Cruz's heart echo the jerky rhythm of her own thunderous pulse as she held him tightly to her. She breathed in the sweet musk of his sweat-sheened skin, loving the warmth of his body and the weight of him pressing her into the mattress. She could have stayed like that, joined with him, for ever. But then he rolled off her without saying a word.

His silence stretched her nerves. She felt hot all over as she replayed her wanton response to him in her mind. Perhaps he was shocked by her shameless enjoyment of sex, unaware that she had only ever behaved with such wild abandon with him? She remembered the deal they had made. He was paying her for sex but perhaps he thought that *she* should pay *him* for servicing her so thoroughly? She risked glancing at him and discovered that he had fallen asleep.

He looked younger and the grooves at the sides of his mouth had disappeared. His dark lashes fanned on his cheeks and his black hair fell across his brow so that Sabrina longed to run her fingers through its silky thickness. In his relaxed state he looked like the younger man she had known ten years ago and she wondered how she had ever had the strength back then to have left him. The painful truth was that he had not loved her and it had been that certainty that had sent her rushing back to Eversleigh, she thought bleakly.

Nothing had changed. He did not love her now. But he had gone to great lengths to make her his mistress despite the fact that he could have any woman he wanted without having to fork out one and a half million pounds. She had been half amused, half irritated at the way the majority of the female guests at the party had openly flirted with him. But Cruz had only had eyes for her, and when he had made love to her just now his primitive hunger had thrilled her because she had known he was powerless to resist the blazing sexual chemistry that sizzled whenever they were near each other.

She bit her lip. At eighteen she had been too young and unsure of herself and too devastated by the miscarriage to fight for him. But making love with him just now had shown her that she still had feelings for him and that maybe—her heart jolted as she tested a startling idea—maybe she had never fallen out of love with him.

So why not fight for him? She would not be the first woman in history to use sex as a way to a man's heart; she thought of her ancestor Henrietta Bancroft who had been the king's mistress.

Her strongest weapon was Cruz's desire for her, but he had insisted that he wanted sex without emotion so that was what she would let him think he was getting. Dared she go through with her plan knowing that six months from now he might walk away from her and break her heart? Her heart had been doomed from the minute he had turned up at Eversleigh Hall, she thought ruefully. If nothing else, she would have six months of amazing sex to remember him by.

The sound of his regular breaths reminded her of when they had been lovers in Brazil and she had lain awake watching him while he slept. She gave in to the temptation to trace her forefinger lightly over his mouth and when he did not stir she moved her hand lower to his chest, following the path of dark hairs that arrowed over his stomach. He took a deeper breath, and she held hers, but he remained asleep and after a moment she continued her exploration, carefully lifting the sheet away from his hips.

He was still semi-aroused, and even in that state the size of his manhood made her breath catch. He was so beautiful, his body honed to perfection and powerfully muscular. Utterly absorbed in her study of him, she could not resist running her fingers over the proud tip of his penis.

His response—to full, hard arousal—was immediate.

'*Deus*, Sabrina, I hope you are prepared to finish what you've started,' Cruz growled.

Her smile made his gut clench. She was an evocative mix of seductive minx and curious innocence that reminded him of the virginal eighteen-year-old who had gifted him with her maidenhood. His thoughts became focused on what she was doing with her hands and he drew a sharp breath when he watched her open a condom and roll it over his throbbing erection.

'I'm prepared, and now so are you,' she murmured. She sat astride him and leaned forwards so that her long blonde hair tumbled in a silken curtain over his chest. 'What is your wish, master?' she said in a teasing voice.

Evidently she had decided to enact the role of concubine. Cruz knew he should respond in the same light tone and join in with her game, but he couldn't. Desire was a ravenous beast inside him that demanded appeasement. How could he be this desperate for her so soon after he'd had sex with her the first time? He despised himself for his inability to resist her, but she leaned further forwards and deliberately stroked her nipples across his chest, and he felt the pressure building inside him until he feared he would explode.

'Kiss me,' he ordered harshly.

When she complied he took her lips, took everything she offered and claimed possession, driving his tongue into her mouth to elicit a sensual exploration that he sensed shocked her with its blatant eroticism. He slid his hands down her spine and shaped the twin globes of her buttocks before he gripped her hips, lifted her high and brought her down onto his erection so that she gasped as her vaginal muscles stretched to accommodate him.

He knew she was surprised by his barely leashed savagery but she did not falter as he encouraged her to ride him. She quickly learned the rhythm he set and the expression on her face became intent as she absorbed thrust after devastating thrust of his solid shaft into her velvet heat.

Faster, faster, Cruz gritted his teeth as he fought to control the primitive urges of his body. He needed her to come now before this went spectacularly wrong, and he was relieved when she gave a sudden sharp cry and he felt her convulse around him. His relief was short-lived as with a sense of disbelief he realised that he could not stop his own release. With a muffled oath he reversed their positions and rolled her beneath him, gave one final, powerful thrust and was hit by a tidal wave of pleasure that went on and on as his seed flooded out of him.

Last night had not been his finest hour, Cruz brooded the following morning. He sat down at the breakfast table but had no appetite for food as his mind replayed his total and humiliating loss of control caused by Sabrina's witchery. He did not understand why she affected him so strongly. With every other woman he'd had sex with he had never had a problem curbing his desire. He could make love for hours, and there had been many occasions when his brain had been occupied with his latest business project while he had gone through the motions of assuring whichever woman was in his bed that she was amazing.

His temper did not improve when Sabrina strolled into the room wearing a short black silk robe that barely covered her thighs. Last night he had ordered her to strip naked and the memory of how she had enjoyed playing the sexual tease evoked a heated sensation in Cruz's groin. She had turned into a wildcat in his arms, but this morning she was a picture of refinement with her blonde hair caught in a knot on top of her head, revealing the slender column of her elegant neck.

As she sat down opposite him at the table he

made a show of glancing at his watch. 'Good morning. Although it's nearly afternoon.' It was an exaggeration but he was irritated that she had evidently had no problem sleeping, while he had stayed awake for most of the night trying to comprehend his craven weakness for her. 'I was about to come and wake you.'

She shrugged. 'I had a bath.'

And she smelled heavenly. Cruz inhaled a waft of rose-scented bath oil and body lotion that she had used to moisturise her skin, and felt a certain part of his anatomy spring to life. 'Would you like coffee?'

'I'd prefer Earl Grey tea if you have it.'

He poured her a cup of anaemic-looking liquid before helping himself to strong black coffee. 'I suppose you are used to a privileged lifestyle where you can get up at whatever time you like instead of having to join the morning commute to a job,' he said tersely.

'Actually my alarm goes off at six a.m. at home. I lecture at a university on two days a week, and if I am commissioned to work on a restoration project I have to travel to London or further afield to a museum or stately home.'

Sabrina frowned. 'I certainly don't swan around at Eversleigh Hall playing the lady of the manor. Running the estate takes up a lot of my time, and anyway I have to get up early to exercise Monty.' Her heart gave a pang as she remembered that her horse would have been collected by his new owner and the stables at Eversleigh would be empty.

Cruz's voice drew her attention back to him and she thought how mouth-wateringly sexy he looked with the top buttons of his shirt open and a shadow of dark stubble on his jaw. Her breasts were a little sore this morning from where his rough jaw had scraped her skin. She forced herself to concentrate on what he was saying.

'When I checked my emails this morning I opened several invitations to social functions addressed to both of us.' Cruz's mouth curled into a cynical smile. 'Many of the newspapers have reported on our romantic liaison, and it would appear that your links with the aristocracy are working in my favour. Perhaps I should marry you,' he said sardonically. 'Having a high-class wife would clearly offer me even more benefits and business opportunities.'

Sabrina's heart missed a beat but her outward response was to raise her finely arched brows. 'I assume you are joking,' she replied in her cultured voice that made Cruz long to ruffle her *sangfroid*.

He watched her take a ripe peach from the fruit bowl and cut it into slivers with a silver knife before she bit into a slice with her perfect white teeth. Juice trickled down her chin and she licked the syrupy liquid with the tip of her tongue. Cruz felt sweat on his brow. *Deus!* Was she deliberately trying to turn him on? He took a gulp of coffee, forgetting that he had just poured it and it was scalding hot. The shock of burning at the back of his throat caused him to jolt and he spilt coffee down the front of his shirt. He swore beneath his breath.

'I know what your reply would be if I had made a serious proposal of marriage,' he said grimly. 'You would turn me down just as you did ten years ago.' His eyes narrowed on her face. 'Or would you?' he mused aloud. 'You didn't want to marry me when I was poor, but now that I am a multimillionaire perhaps you would consider me a better catch. Why settle for one and a half million pounds when, if you were my wife, you could get your claws on my entire fortune?'

Sabrina pushed her half-eaten peach away. For some reason Cruz was being deliberately insulting. She did not know why he was in a foul mood, but perhaps he had tired of her already and was regretting paying her to be his mistress. She knew full well that he hadn't been serious about wanting to marry her.

'Your lack of money wasn't the reason I turned you down. *It wasn't,*' she insisted when he gave a disbelieving laugh. 'It was because you had asked me to marry you for the wrong reason.'

'You were expecting my baby.'

'Exactly. You wanted your child, not me.'

'Deus.' He slammed his hand down on the

table. 'We both had a duty to do the best for our child.'

'I don't believe a shotgun wedding is in the best interests of a child, and I should know because I am the product of such a marriage. Most of the time, my parents couldn't even be civil to one another.'

'You were eighteen, I'd got you pregnant through my carelessness the one occasion I failed to use protection and I was trying to do the right thing,' Cruz said frustratedly. 'Why don't you be honest and admit that you felt trapped when you fell pregnant?'

'I did not resent my pregnancy,' Sabrina insisted. 'But it changed things between us. You were angry that I refused to marry you, and you stopped making love to me, I assumed because you found my pregnancy a turn-off.'

'It wasn't that.' Cruz was stunned by Sabrina's revelation. He recalled the nights when he had lain next to her in his small bed at his parents' cottage and fought his overwhelming desire to make love to her. 'My mother had explained that it wasn't safe for us to have sex once you were pregnant.'

Sabrina remembered that Cruz had said his mother had suffered numerous miscarriages, which might have made her believe in the old wives' tale. 'Pregnancy is not an illness. Millions of women continue with their ordinary daily activities during pregnancy, including having sex. If you had talked to me rather than your mother we might have avoided many of the misunderstandings that came between us,' she said bitterly. 'Don't you think it's ironic that we are finally talking about our relationship ten years after it ended?'

She jumped up from the table and marched into the adjoining bedroom, feeling frustrated that so much had been unsaid between them ten years ago. But perhaps if she had stayed in Brazil instead of rushing back to Eversleigh Hall they might have stood a chance of resolving their differences. In hindsight she could see that she had been as much to blame as Cruz for the breakdown in communication between them.

She heard him follow her into the bedroom.

'Talking wasn't part of our relationship, was it?' She sighed. 'The truth is that we barely knew each other when I became pregnant. Up until then we had just had sex, a lot of sex, but sex wasn't enough to build a relationship on ten years ago and it isn't enough now.'

'Well, fortunately I don't want to build a relationship.'

Something in Cruz's tone sent a ripple of warning down Sabrina's spine and she glanced over at him to see him shrug out of his coffee-stained shirt and screw it into a ball.

Sabrina had almost sounded convincing when she had said that the reason she had refused to marry him was because she had been affected by her parents' unhappy marriage, Cruz brooded. But he knew it wasn't the truth. He was convinced that she had rejected him because he had not been rich and successful. She had decided that he was not good enough for her and she had made him feel that his love wasn't good enough.

It seemed to be a recurring theme, he thought

grimly. He had adored his father, but deep in his heart he felt that Vitor had cared more about finding a flawless diamond than he'd cared about his family. Although Cruz blamed Earl Bancroft for his father's accident, the painful truth was that Vitor's obsession with diamonds had contributed to his death. Cruz had been left to care for his mother and sisters, and he had tried, *Deus*, he had tried so hard to comfort his mother. But she had been inconsolable, and once again Cruz had felt that whatever he did and however hard he worked to support his family, it was not enough to lift his mother from her grief.

His jaw hardened. Sabrina had ripped his heart out when she had left him years ago, but there was no chance that she would hurt him again.

'When you lost the baby it gave you the excuse to return to your precious Eversleigh Hall and a luxurious lifestyle that you were never going to have with a miner from a *favela*,' he accused her harshly. 'Ten years ago you thought that all I was good enough for was sex. Now our situations are reversed and all I want from you is sex, a lot of sex,' he mimicked her words. 'That's what I paid you for.'

Sabrina's eyes clashed with his glittering gaze as she watched him walk towards her. 'What do you think you're doing?' It was a stupid question, she acknowledged. Cruz's sculpted features had hardened with sexual intent that sent a quiver of anticipation through her. It had been the same when they had first met in Brazil, she thought ruefully. They had ripped each other's clothes off at every opportunity and had explosive sex.

'Cruz…' She held out her hand as if to ward him off, but she knew as well as he did that it was a token protest. Excitement licked like wildfire through her veins as he unbuckled his belt and in a few deft movements rid himself of his trousers, shoes and socks and lastly the black silk boxers that had been unable to disguise his powerful erection.

He flicked open the belt of her robe, stripped her and scooped her into his arms. In two strides he reached the bed and dropped her onto the mattress. She really could not let him dominate her like this, Sabrina told herself, but he thwarted her attempt to slide across the bed by pushing her flat on her back and with firm hands took hold of her ankles, hooking her legs over his shoulders.

'I'm not interested in the past,' he told her. 'All I'm interested in is finding the map of the diamond mine that I'm sure your father hid somewhere in Eversleigh Hall. You sold yourself to me and I will hold you to your agreement to be my mistress for six months, whether you like it or not.' He smiled down at her flushed face. 'But you do like it, don't you, *gatinha*? From your response to me last night I bet you have never found another man who can satisfy you like I can.'

Sabrina wanted to deny his arrogant boast, but she couldn't, damn him. Desire coiled in the pit of her stomach and she arched her hips as he lowered his mouth to her feminine heart. His warm breath stirred the tight blonde curls between her thighs and she shuddered with longing. But he made her wait with her legs spread wide, waiting for him to run his tongue up and down her moist opening before he finally gave in to her husky plea and bestowed a shockingly intimate caress that drove her swiftly to the edge of ecstasy.

He used his fingers to keep her there while he sheathed himself and then he penetrated her with a slow, deep thrust that filled her, completed her. She wrapped her arms around his back as he began to move, driving into her with a steady rhythm that devastated her. Cruz remained in complete control while she writhed and moaned beneath him, and Sabrina, remembering her decision the previous night to fight for him and try to win his heart, wondered despairingly if he even had a heart.

CHAPTER NINE

THEY DROVE TO Eversleigh Hall that afternoon. Sabrina remained silent for the journey, feeling mortified as she remembered how she had lost all her inhibitions and come apart utterly when Cruz had made love to her. Thankfully he had headed into the en-suite immediately after he had withdrawn his body from hers and by the time he had emerged after taking a shower she had managed to hide her shattered emotions behind a mask of cool composure.

'I want to start searching for the map immediately,' he told her as they walked into the house. 'We won't be able to spend much time in Surrey because I have work and social commitments in London and various other European cities.'

Sabrina frowned. 'Surely you don't expect me to get involved in your business dealings? Why can't I stay here while you travel abroad?'

'The point of paying you to be my mistress is that you will be available whenever I want you,' he said silkily.

She bristled at his arrogant assumption that he could simply take over her life. 'I thought I had explained that I have a job at the local university, and I also do freelance work restoring antique furniture. My career is important to me and my commitment to my role as a lecturer is non-negotiable.'

'Perhaps I should remind you that you are not in a position to negotiate anything. For the next six months your only commitment is to your role as my mistress. I will also need you to show me the secret hiding places where your father might have put the map.'

She flushed at his reminder that she had sold herself to him. It occurred to her that if the map was found quickly, Cruz would presumably return to his diamond mine in Brazil and hopefully he would leave her in peace. 'I'll give you a tour of the house,' she said coolly, somehow managing to disguise the riot of emotions inside her. 'We'll start in the library.'

Sabrina swept past him, and Cruz cursed beneath his breath. She did not have to look so wounded, damn it. He had given her the means to save her precious stately home so why the hell did he feel so goddamned guilty? He followed her into the library. 'Which days do you work at the university?'

'Tuesdays and Wednesdays, but I didn't work this week because it is a reading week for the students.'

He shrugged. 'Most of our social engagements are at weekends, and it is likely that we will stay at Eversleigh during the week, meaning that you will be able to fulfil your lecturing contract.'

Sabrina shot him a startled look. Cruz almost sounded as though he understood that her career meant a lot to her. It was all she had that alleviated the burden of responsibility she felt for Eversleigh, she thought bleakly. She had a flashback to the first night he had paid an unexpected visit to the hall. When he had kissed her she'd felt as though he had brought her back to life after she had merely existed for the ten years that they had been apart. She suddenly wished that they could have met again simply as two people who were attracted to each other instead of them playing a strange game of blame and revenge.

She walked over to where he was standing by the window and followed his gaze over the immaculately kept gardens and the view of the beautiful Surrey countryside.

'I'm not surprised that you wanted to rush back here rather than live with me in a run-down miner's cottage in Brazil,' he commented. 'It must have been an incredible place to grow up.'

Sabrina was silent for a moment, thinking of her lonely childhood. Cruz believed that her life had been perfect. When they had been lovers he had been sensitive about what he had perceived as the difference in their social status. She wished she could make him understand that having money did not equate to happiness.

'I realise I was lucky to live in a big house and I attended the best schools. But although I had material things, I didn't have what you had.' He gave her a sardonic look and she knew he was thinking that she lived in a luxurious stately home while he had grown up in a Brazilian slum. 'Your parents loved you and made you feel part of a family,' she reminded him. 'My brother and I were mainly cared for by nannies. My father was rarely at Eversleigh, and even before my mother left us she was busy with her own life.'

She moved across the room and slid open one of the wooden wall panels. 'This is a priest hole where Catholic priests used to hide hundreds of years ago when they were persecuted for their faith. Tristan and I called it the choker,' she explained when Cruz put his head inside the cramped, dark space. 'One particularly unkind nanny who came to look after us used to lock us in here as a punishment. When the panel is closed no light can get in. I didn't care so much, but Tristan used to be terrified.'

'Why didn't you tell your parents that the nanny was guilty of physical and mental child cruelty?'

'My mother had moved to France, and my father spent most of his time in Brazil.' Sabrina gave a rueful smile. 'The nanny didn't stay at Eversleigh for long. Tristan put a grass snake in her bed and she left the next day. He did it because the nanny had upset me,' she explained. 'Tris had never seen me cry before. When I was a young child I learned not to show my emotions because my father couldn't abide what he called snivelling and self-pity. But the nanny had said that my mother had moved away because she obviously didn't love me…' her voice faltered '…and I realised it was the truth.'

She shut the panel and looked at Cruz. 'You often point out that I had a privileged upbringing but the reality is that I felt lonely and unloved during my childhood. I never felt a close emotional bond with my parents.'

Cruz was shocked by Sabrina's revelations about her upbringing. The picture she had painted did not match the image he had of her as a spoiled princess who had wanted for nothing and who had believed that he was not good enough for her ten years ago. Was it possible that he had misjudged her? He pushed the unwelcome thought away.

'Am I supposed to feel sorry for you, poor little rich girl?' he mocked. 'In the *favela*, the shack where I lived as a boy had two tiny rooms and no electricity or running water. I never even saw a green space or a flower. The piece of rough ground where I used to play with the other slum kids had an open sewer running next to it, but after a while you get used to the stench,' he said grimly.

His jaw hardened. 'My father worked in the diamond mine because he wanted to earn money to give his family the chance of a better life. But he paid with his own life because your wealthy, privileged father sent him into an area of the mine that he knew was dangerous.'

Sabrina's temper flared. 'You are so sure that my father was responsible for the accident, but he isn't here to defend himself and so I must. I don't believe he would have deliberately put the men who worked in his mine at risk. I admit he wasn't the best father to me and my brother but he was, *is*,' she corrected herself because she had to believe the earl would return to Eversleigh, 'an honourable man. I'm desperately sorry that your father died, but perhaps there is another explanation for his death.'

'What explanation could there be?' Cruz demanded.

'It must be wonderful to have your supreme self-assurance and the belief that only you can be right,' she said bitterly. 'You refuse to listen, and it was the same ten years ago. You were adamant that we should marry when I became pregnant, even though we didn't really know each other.'

Cruz struggled to control his anger. He *knew* she had refused to marry him because he had lacked money or a title and it infuriated him that she could not be honest. 'It was my responsibility to take care of you and our child.'

'The fact that we can't have a discussion without it turning into a row proves that if we *had* married it would have been a disaster. We can't talk to each other,' she said flatly.

'I've always thought that talking was overrated.' The hard gleam in Cruz's eyes as he walked towards her sent a frisson of mingled desire and despair down Sabrina's spine. 'There are far more enjoyable ways in which we can communicate that don't involve talking. The first night I arrived at Eversleigh we both imagined having sex on this desk.'

He began to unbutton his shirt, revealing his hair-roughened chest. Sabrina felt her body's instinctive response and she knew without looking down that her nipples had hardened and were jutting provocatively through her blouse. She closed her eyes to block out his mocking expression.

'Now seems a good time to fulfil at least one of our fantasies,' he drawled.

If he touched her she would be lost, and not just physically, she acknowledged painfully. If he insisted on sex because he had paid for the privilege, his cold cynicism would destroy her fragile defences, and she could not risk him guessing how she felt about him.

Pride and a stubborn determination learned during her childhood, to keep her emotions hidden, brought her chin up. 'I would have thought that your first priority is to find the map of the diamond mine that is so important to you. Anything else,' she said in a faintly bored tone, 'can wait, can't it?'

Did anything touch her? Cruz wondered savagely, aware that every muscle on his body was taut with rampant desire that was humiliatingly out of his control. Sabrina was the archetypal lady of the manor, crisply elegant in beautifully tailored cream trousers and a pale pink blouse, the pearls at her throat reflecting the translucence of her skin. He knew he could have her bent over the desk and she would be with him all the way. Their sexual compatibility was one thing that had never been in doubt. But her eyes were as dark as storm clouds and he glimpsed a shadow of vulnerability in their grey depths that stopped him from pulling her into his arms.

With an effort he stemmed the hot tide of lust surging through his veins, but curiously as he moved away from her he found himself wishing that he could simply hold her until the shadows in her eyes disappeared.

'As you say, searching for the map is my top priority. In Brazil, Diego is keen to know if we will have to close the diamond mine, or if we can extend operations into a previously abandoned section of the mine that I am convinced exists.'

'How is Diego, these days?' Sabrina seized the opportunity to turn the focus away from the sexual tension that was almost tangible between them.

'Diego is—Diego.' Cruz smiled wryly as he thought of his close friend from the *favela*. One thing he was certain of was that Diego Cazorra would never allow himself to be affected by a woman, however beautiful she might be.

'I thought he owned the diamond mine in partnership with you.'

'Diego is in charge of the day-to-day operating of the mine and I concentrate on selling the diamonds we find on the international market. Three years ago I established Delgado Diamonds, and Diego has several business projects of his own and is a successful gold prospector.' Cruz looked amused. 'The Cazorra philosophy is to work hard and play harder.'

A knock on the door was a welcome interruption and Sabrina turned her attention to the butler. 'The builders have arrived to give a quote on the cost of repairing the fire damage to the annexe, Miss Sabrina,' John informed her.

'I'll come and talk to them,' she murmured and hurried out of the library, flushing hotly as she heard Cruz call after her mockingly.

'We'll wait until later to try out the desk, *gatinha*.'

Another social function—the third that week, Cruz reflected as he fastened the cuff links on his white dinner shirt. Tonight's party was a black-tie event taking place at a five-star hotel not far from Eversleigh Hall. The charity fundraising dinner would be followed by a private fashion show by one of the leading design houses, and the models would be wearing jewellery for the evening provided by Delgado Diamonds.

Business at the new Bond Street store was booming, and, since the launch party a month ago, profits had outstripped all of Cruz's expectations. He knew his very public affair with Sabrina was responsible for the huge media interest, both in them as a couple and in his jewellery company. Sabrina's connections to the British aristocracy had given Cruz acceptance into the most exclusive social circles. And he could have no complaints about the way she was fulfilling the other part of their deal, he acknowledged.

For the past month she had played the role of his mistress faultlessly. She accompanied him to parties elegantly dressed in haute couture, and she was always a charming and interesting companion with a broad knowledge of current affairs and a genuine enthusiasm for her specialist subjects of history and the arts. They either stayed in Kensington or at Eversleigh Hall, although they did not sleep in Sabrina's bedroom.

Cruz had taken one look at the candy-pink walls and the large collection of teddy bears piled on the bed and commented that the room looked as if it had been decorated for a child.

'My mother helped me choose the colour

scheme when I was ten,' she had admitted. 'The room reminds me of her, and I don't want to get rid of my bears. After Mum left, they and Tristan were my best friends.'

The image of Sabrina living virtually on her own in the huge house with only a nanny to look after her had evoked a strange tug in Cruz's heart, but he had ignored the unwelcome sensation. He'd chosen another bear-free bedroom for them to share and added a few toys of his own, namely a mirror fitted to the ceiling above the bed, and a pair of diamond-encrusted handcuffs, which he had persuaded Sabrina to wear the first time and she had asked him to use on several occasions since.

Whoever had coined the idiom 'be careful what you wish for' had known what they were talking about, he mused. When Sabrina had agreed to be his mistress he had insisted that all he wanted was sex without emotion—and that was exactly what she gave him every night.

Their enormous four-poster bed at Eversleigh Hall was their sensual playground where they shut out the world and indulged in long hours of lovemaking that left them sated until the morning, when he would reach across the mattress for her and she would slide into his arms, as hungry for sex as he was.

But afterwards she always moved back to her side of the bed. It was as if there were an invisible barrier between them, and with each passing day, and night, Cruz felt a growing sense of frustration that had nothing to do with his sexual appetite. He found himself wishing that she would remain in his arms after they'd had sex, even though he had always been irritated by previous lovers who had wanted to cuddle and cling to him, or, even worse, wanted him to talk to them.

There were no such problems with Sabrina. She would reply if he initiated conversation, and she was perfectly pleasant and cordial, but her air of detachment made him want to shake a response from her. Even in bed, when her desire matched his and she responded to him with a fervency that drove him to the edge of his sanity, he sensed that she held some part of herself back from him.

He should be pleased, Cruz told himself, that when their business deal ended five months from now and he no longer required her to be his mistress, he would not have to worry that she might make a scene when he walked away from her. In fact, she probably would not even notice that he had gone.

He turned towards the door as she emerged from her dressing room, and the faint tug on his heart became a hard ache. The full-length, strapless evening gown, the colour of deep red wine, fitted her like a glove and showed off her tiny waist while the ruched bodice pushed her breasts high and gave her a deep cleavage that Cruz knew would draw the eyes of every male at the party.

'You look exquisite,' he murmured, hoping she did not hear the raw note of longing in his voice. He picked up a slim leather box from the dressing table and walked over to her. 'I have something for you to wear that I think will suit your dress perfectly.'

Sabrina caught her breath as Cruz opened the lid to reveal a single strand of square-cut diamonds that even though she was no expert she could tell were of exceptional quality. The diamonds glittered with a fiery brilliance as he lifted the necklace out of the box and held it against her skin.

'Turn round and lift up your hair.'

Pleasure shivered through her when she felt his fingers lightly brush against the back of her neck as he fastened the necklace. He looked unbelievably gorgeous in his formal dinner suit and she wished the evening were over and she could undress him slowly, tease him a little so that he promised punishment in return. Perhaps he would order her to lie face down on the pillows and use the diamond handcuffs to secure her hands to the ornate Victorian bedhead. She felt a familiar molten sensation between her legs. Cruz had revealed a depth of sensuality to her nature that she had not known existed and she was certain she would never experience with any other man, she thought bleakly.

'What do you think?'

'What?' She was startled out of her reverie and prayed he had no idea of her wayward thoughts. 'Oh…it's beautiful.' She touched the diamond necklace that circled her throat. 'This must be the loveliest piece in the Delgado collection and I'll enjoy showcasing it for you tonight. I'm sure it will attract plenty of interest from potential buyers at the party.'

'It's not a Delgado piece. I commissioned the necklace using stones from my own personal collection, and it's not for sale, it's a gift for you.'

Her heart gave a jolt. 'I can't possibly accept something so valuable.' She spun round to face him and saw an indefinable emotion briefly cross his sculpted features. 'You have already given me the means to safeguard my home,' she said huskily. 'I don't ask or want for more.'

'You didn't want to save Eversleigh for yourself. You wanted it for your brother, didn't you? I am aware of how titles and estates are passed down the generations of a family through the male line.' Cruz cut her off before she could argue. 'I also discovered from Tristan when he visited last week that he is about to begin the very expensive training course to become a commercial airline pilot. Your brother was under the impression that the course fees were paid out of your father's bank account, but you and I know differently, don't we, *querida*?'

'You didn't tell Tris the truth, did you?' she asked sharply.

'Of course I didn't. But I wish you had been more honest with me. You allowed me to think that you wanted to continue living a life of luxury at Eversleigh Hall, but instead I find that you are responsible for running the house and estate and you do everything from mopping floors to mending farm fences.'

She shrugged. 'What difference would it have made if you had known the situation here? I still needed money to keep the estate solvent until my father returns.' Her grey eyes met his olive-green gaze, and she said quietly, 'There was only one reason why I sold my body to you.'

She meant Eversleigh of course, Cruz told himself. He raked a hand through his hair. 'If I'd known you were offering yourself as a martyr for your family I would have…I don't know…been kinder, more caring.' Dull colour ran under his skin when Sabrina stared at him.

'Caring is an emotion, but all you want from me is sex. You can't change the rules halfway through the game.' She threw her pashmina around her shoulders. 'It's time we were going, or we'll be late.'

Cruz inhaled her perfume, a subtle blend of white orchids and jasmine, as elegantly beautiful as the woman wearing it, and he was tempted to haul her into his arms and tell her that it was his game and he could change the rules whenever he liked. But Sabrina had already stepped into the hallway and she stooped down to scoop a ball of ginger fur into her arms.

'Darling George, I won't be gone for too long,' she crooned to the cat. 'I hope you don't miss me, sweetheart.'

'I'm sure he'll survive on his own for a few hours.' Cruz told himself it was ridiculous to feel jealous of a cat. He and George had come to a truce of sorts, in that he tolerated the cat, and the cat gave him a smug look every time it jumped into Sabrina's lap.

'You are so heartless,' she complained when he firmly closed the door to deny the cat access to the bedroom. 'I love George.'

'Lucky George,' Cruz murmured.

As he followed Sabrina down the stairs he realised that he could not allow this unsatisfactory situation to continue. He had set the rules of their relationship and he could change them, but first he needed to be clear about what he wanted from his infuriatingly aloof mistress.

CHAPTER TEN

IF SOMEONE HAD told him when he had been growing up in the *favela,* forced to search through piles of rotting rubbish for something to eat, that one day he would be bored of champagne and caviar, he would have found it hugely funny, Cruz brooded.

He kept his thoughts to himself and smiled at the silver-haired woman beside him who seemed to have been talking for hours. Lady Aisling's husband had business connections in China, and networking was always useful. The chance to socialise with powerful business leaders was the reason Cruz had coerced Sabrina into being his mistress. One of the reasons, he acknowledged self-derisively as his gaze was drawn to her. She looked stunning in her figure-hugging velvet gown, and she was clearly charming the socks off Lord Aisling.

Sabrina's beautiful face was animated and she exuded an air of warm friendliness that drew people to her. Why did she never smile at him the way she was smiling at Lord Aisling, or the waiter who stopped to offer her a tray of canapés? She showed more affection to her goddamned cat than to him, Cruz thought darkly. But as she had reminded him, emotions were not included in their deal.

Lady Aisling's voice pulled him from his thoughts. 'Charles and I are driving down to Chichester tomorrow to spend a few days on our yacht. Do you have any plans for the bank holiday weekend, Mr Delgado?'

'Actually I've arranged to take Sabrina to my house in Portugal.'

'This is the first time you have mentioned your plans to me, darling,' Sabrina said sweetly while her eyes flashed daggers at Cruz.

'I wanted to surprise you—darling.'

'Oh, you have,' she murmured in a syrupy tone that didn't fool him for a minute.

He deemed it sensible to keep out of her line of fire for the rest of the evening. The party was a lavish affair, the food was divine and the vintage champagne superb, but Cruz could not throw off his black mood. He had everything he had ever dreamed of as a boy: money, several beautiful houses in various parts of the world and, perhaps more important than anything, financial security that enabled him to take care of his mother and sisters. He also currently went to bed every night with a stunning blonde who had proved herself willing to satisfy his every sexual whim, so why the hell wasn't he happy?

'How long do you plan for us to spend in Portugal?' Sabrina demanded after the party had ended and they were travelling back to Eversleigh Hall in the chauffeur-driven Bentley.

'A week or two.'

'A week or *two*! May I remind you that I have a job? My lectures at the university—'

'Have been rescheduled for next month,' Cruz told her blandly. 'I phoned the principal and explained that I needed to arrange for you to have special leave. Mrs Peters thought it was very romantic,' he added drily.

'Presumably you didn't disillusion her and tell

her that the only reason you require my presence in Portugal is to provide you with sex?' Sabrina snapped. She felt furious that Cruz thought he owned her, although technically for the next five months he did, she conceded.

At the end of their business arrangement he would walk away from her. The thought hurt more than it had any right to. Each time they made love she found it harder to hide her emotional response to him, but she knew she must, because Cruz was not interested in her emotions. All he wanted from her was convenient sex while he was at Eversleigh to search for the map that had so far proved elusive.

She glanced at his chiselled profile and thought that he did not look particularly happy. Her heart lurched. Had he grown tired of their arrangement and bored of her? He had been in a curious mood all evening, and several times during the party she had caught him looking at her with an unfathomable expression in his eyes.

'Tell me about your parents,' he said unexpectedly. 'You gave the impression that they hated each other.'

It was the first time since she had become his mistress that he had shown any curiosity about her personal life. 'I don't think they felt such a strong emotion as hate,' Sabrina said slowly, 'but they grew to dislike each other intensely. My mother told me that they had only dated a few times when she fell pregnant with me. I was very much an accident, but my grandfather, who was the earl at that time, insisted that my father married my mother, and threatened to disinherit him if he refused. My father stood at the altar with a figurative gun aimed at his head. It was hardly a good start, and the marriage deteriorated rapidly when Dad started spending most of his time in Brazil.'

'I don't understand how you can compare our situation ten years ago with your parents,' Cruz said harshly. 'No one forced me to propose to you.'

'You only asked me because I was carrying your baby. There was a good chance that if we had married we would have ended up arguing constantly like I remember my parents doing, and like we seem to do now. We don't discuss things,' Sabrina muttered. 'You lay down the law and expect me to comply. The trip to Portugal that you've decided on is a prime example of how you are determined to have your own way and you ride roughshod over my feelings.'

Cruz raked a hand through his hair. He was unused to being verbally crucified and he did not like the experience. 'That was not my intention.' Honesty forced him to acknowledge there was some truth in Sabrina's words.

'I suppose I might seem controlling sometimes,' he said grudgingly. 'After my father died I became responsible for my mother and sisters. Graciana and Jacinta were just ten years old and they missed their *papai* terribly. My mother crumbled without Vitor. She relied on me to earn money to keep the family and make all the decisions about my sisters' upbringing. In effect I became a substitute father to the twins.'

Sabrina reflected that some aspects of their lives mirrored each other's. 'It was the same for me when my parents divorced and I felt that I had to take care of my brother,' she admitted.

The car drew up outside Eversleigh Hall and as they walked into the house she murmured, 'Do you realise that was the first time we have talked about the past without it turning into an argument with accusations on both sides?'

Cruz had been thinking the same thing. He recalled Sabrina had said that if they had talked more ten years ago maybe there would have been fewer misunderstandings between them. But when he had first met her he had been younger and less self-assured than he was now. He had been tormented with insecurity that he was a poorly paid manual labourer while Sabrina came from an aristocratic family and was used to a luxurious standard of living. It was true that they had not talked much, but he had shown her how he felt about her every time they had made love, he thought defensively.

When Sabrina had fallen pregnant he had not risked initiating sex because he had believed it could be dangerous for her and their unborn child.

He put his hand on her arm as she was about to walk up the stairs. 'Will you join me in the library for a nightcap?' He saw her look of surprise. Usually he liked to have a drink while he checked his business emails before he joined her in bed. 'I'm beginning to realise that you were right when you said that we needed to talk about what happened ten years ago,' he said roughly.

He poured whisky into two glasses, added lemonade to one, knowing it was how Sabrina preferred it, and handed her drink to her before he joined her on the sofa.

'I accept that I was perhaps overly protective of you while you were pregnant,' he admitted. 'Growing up in the *favela*, my experiences of women in pregnancy were mostly bad and led me to believe that childbirth was potentially life-threatening for both mother and infant. Recently there have been improvements in health and social care for the poorest of Brazil's population but twenty years ago it was a different story. My mother almost died during one of her pregnancies. I remember when I was about twelve years old Mamãe miscarried late in her pregnancy. She lost so much blood and I thought she could not possibly survive.'

'It must have been a frightening experience for you.' Sabrina was appalled as she tried to imagine the terrible scene Cruz had witnessed when he had been a boy. 'Were you concerned for our baby during my pregnancy?'

'I was terrified for you and the child. When I came up from the mineshaft and was told that you were in hospital and had been bleeding heavily, it was like I had fallen back into a nightmare, only it was you instead of my mother whose life was in danger, and my own child not a sibling whose life was over before it had begun.'

A lump formed in Sabrina's throat. 'I thought you were angry with me. You hardly spoke after the miscarriage, and you avoided looking at me.'

'I felt guilty.' Cruz's jaw clenched. 'If you had died, it would have been my fault. You had told me you felt unwell that morning and I should have stayed with you instead of going to work.

But I needed to earn money. In a few months there was going to be a new mouth to feed, and I was determined that my child would never go hungry like I often did when I was growing up.'

'I wish you had told me how you had been affected by your mother's experiences. It would have helped me to understand why you acted the way you did when I became pregnant.' Sabrina bit her lip. 'I'd hoped you would come to Eversleigh after me. I was unaware that your father had died.'

'I assumed when I didn't hear from you after Vitor's death that you didn't want anything more to do with me.' Cruz looked at her intently. 'If you had known about my father would you have come back to Brazil?'

'Of course I would have done. It makes me sad to think that you were on your own trying to help your mother and sisters through their grief while you were grieving for your father.'

Something tight and hard inside Cruz softened a little. He finished his Scotch and caught Sabrina's hand in his. 'Let's go to bed.' He watched her eyes turn smoky with a desire that matched his own. 'I arranged the trip to Portugal because you were right about us needing to lay the past to rest. My villa is beautiful and secluded, but more importantly it represents neutral territory that holds no painful memories for either of us. Maybe at Quinta na Floresta we will find the courage to be honest with each other so that we can both move forwards with our lives.'

Cruz's villa was situated in the stunning Sintra National Park on the west coast of Portugal. On the half-hour journey from Lisbon in his open-topped sports car they drove past miles of golden beaches on one side, and verdant forest on the other.

The feel of the warm sun on her face and the wind blowing her hair helped to ease Sabrina's tension. It was the first time she had been away from Eversleigh for months, and, although she loved her home, she realised that the responsibility of running the estate had become a burden. Since the plane had landed in Portugal she had felt a sense of freedom and excitement at sharing a holiday with Cruz. Sun, sea and plenty of sex were guaranteed! But she also hoped that on neutral territory they would be able to set aside the hostility and resentment that had simmered between them in England.

'The landscape is breathtaking,' she commented. 'It's amazing that dense woodland grows so close to the coastline.'

'This area of Portugal is known historically as the place where the land ends and the sea begins. The national park boasts some of the most spectacular scenery in the world.'

She gave a sideways glance at Cruz and thought that he looked pretty spectacular in his designer shades, with his dark hair tousled by the wind as the car raced along the coastal highway. 'What made you choose to buy a house in Portugal? Was it because Portuguese is the national language in Brazil?'

'The language was one factor. I brought my mother here to visit her sister and she felt immediately at home. Mamãe speaks very little English, but that's not a problem for her here.

I wanted to base myself in Europe and I fell in love with Quinta na Floresta.'

Cruz turned the car onto a long gravel driveway and Sabrina caught her breath when the house came into view. 'When you said you owned a villa I wasn't expecting a palace.'

He laughed. 'It was actually a palace originally, built by a bishop back in the sixteenth century. The building has been updated many times over the years but many of the historic features remain. The olive grove is over two hundred years old and there are forty acres of vineyards. I plan to retire here one day and spend my days inspecting my grapes and drinking fine wine.'

'I can understand why you would never want to leave,' Sabrina murmured as she climbed out of the car and looked at the house. The walls were painted cream and the shutters at the windows were soft olive-green, contrasting with the terracotta roof tiles. Exotic trees and shrubs with vividly coloured flowers stood against the dense blue sky. Encircling the house was a wide moat and access to the front door was over a pretty white stone bridge.

Cruz led the way across a cool marble-floored entrance hall, off which there were numerous elegant rooms decorated in muted pastel shades. As they passed a glass-roofed garden room Sabrina glimpsed the deep blue of a swimming pool beyond the French doors. She followed him outside and discovered that the villa had been built around a central courtyard. At its centre was an ornamental pool and magnificent fountain that sent jets of water shooting high into the sky.

'I love how the spray is cooling on your skin,' she said, stepping closer to the fountain. 'This is just lovely. It's so peaceful here, as if the rest of the world doesn't exist.' She leaned forward, intrigued by the pattern carved all around the central stone plinth of the fountain, and her heart missed a beat. 'It says...*Luiz*.' Deep inside her she felt as though a knot were being tightened.

'I commissioned the fountain to be built soon after I bought the house, as a memorial to our son.'

'But—how did you know that I had given him the name Luiz?' she said huskily.

'I *didn't* know you had named the baby.' Cruz's eyes narrowed on her suddenly pale face. 'You showed no emotion after the miscarriage and you seemed impatient to return to England. I assumed you wanted to forget everything that had happened and get on with the plans you had made before we met. Although our son had never lived, I knew I would never forget about him and in my heart I called him Luiz.'

The knot inside Sabrina pulled tighter. 'I will never forget him either. Sometimes I wonder what he would be like if he had lived. I wish…' She broke off and swallowed in an effort to ease the ache in her throat. She felt Cruz move closer to her, but she dared not look at him, afraid she would see anger on his face, blame that she should have taken better care of their child when he had been developing inside her.

'What do you wish?'

'It doesn't matter.' She could not bring herself to tell him that she wished she could turn the clock back to the day four months into her pregnancy when she had made the fateful decision to ride her horse. She would never know if it had been the reason for the miscarriage but her sense of guilt would always haunt her.

Lost in her thoughts, Sabrina watched the droplets of water from the fountain cascade through the air and sparkle like diamonds in the sunlight. She felt moisture on her face and knew it was tears, not spray, that she wiped from her cheeks with trembling fingers.

'The fountain is a beautiful memorial to our son,' she said huskily.

Cruz stared at Sabrina's drawn features. She looked fragile, as if being reminded of the child they had lost had hurt her. If she had not wanted their baby as he had supposed, would she look so shattered? Her raw emotions as she stood in front of the fountain were palpable and made him question his belief that she had not been as devastated as he had by the miscarriage ten years ago.

She gave him a tremulous smile and he felt a tug on his heart when he noticed the shimmer of tears in her eyes. 'I'd love to explore the villa.'

'I'll give you a tour of the house later. I told my mother I would bring you to meet her as soon as we arrived.'

'Does your mother live here?'

'Not in the main villa. She has her own house that I had built for her in the grounds and my sisters share another house. Jacinta and Graciana are looking forward to meeting you.'

Time and grief had left their mark on Ana-Maria Delgado and Sabrina hardly recognised the white-haired woman who greeted her in halting English. Cruz's twin sisters had been little girls when Sabrina had last seen them, and she remembered that they had been shy and unable to speak any English. She was surprised when Cruz introduced two beautiful, articulate, multilingual young women who were studying at university. Jacinta explained that she planned to be a doctor, and Graciana hoped to graduate as a lawyer.

'It is because of Cruz that we can look forward to good careers,' Graciana told Sabrina over dinner at the twins' house. A large crowd sat around the table. Cruz's aunt and uncle and several cousins had been invited to the meal. 'We owe our brother so much,' Graciana explained. 'After Papai died Cruz worked tirelessly to support us and our mother. But more than simply providing money so that we could enjoy a good standard of living, he took care of all of us and he acted like a father to me and Jacinta.' She grinned at her older brother. 'Sometimes he can be *too* protective. He interviews our boyfriends so thoroughly that he frightens them off.'

'Would you rather I allowed you to date unsuitable men?' Cruz queried. His tone became serious. 'That will never happen, *bonita*. I would protect my little sisters with my life if necessary.'

Jacinta laughed. 'Graciana and I realise it will take a brave man who will not be overawed by our brother.' She waited until Cruz had turned his head to speak to another of his relatives before she said in a fierce voice to Sabrina, 'Cruz is an amazing, wonderful person and he deserves a very special woman who will love him as much as his family loves him.'

Fortunately the arrival of dessert—a Brazilian sweet milk pudding called *pudim de leite*—turned attention away from Sabrina. She glanced around the table at Cruz laughing with his sisters and cousins and thought of her solitary mealtimes in the grand dining room at Eversleigh Hall. She had plenty of friends who often came to stay, and of course Tristan was good company when he was home from university. But she had never experienced the bond that existed between Cruz and his family and she felt like an outsider who did not belong in his close-knit circle.

The twins clearly adored him, and Cruz's love for his mother and sisters was evident in the warmth of his voice. He looked more relaxed than Sabrina had ever seen him and she felt a stab of envy every time he laughed and joked with his family. She remembered how, in the early days of their relationship ten years ago, they had shared laughter and friendship as well as passion and her heart ached for everything she had lost. Not just her child but the man she had loved—and would always love, she realised—but who had never loved her.

If he had cared for her at all he would have tried to persuade her not to leave Brazil. He would have fought for her as he had fought to look after his mother and sisters. Cruz had worked so hard for his family and he was still determined to protect them. Sabrina blinked away the tears that suddenly blinded her. To all appearances she had a privileged life and wanted for nothing, but what she wanted more than anything was to be cherished and protected, to be *loved* by Cruz, who she had discovered was a truly wonderful and honourable man.

'Your sisters are a credit to you,' she told him later when they strolled past lemon and olive groves on the way back to his villa. 'Jacinta told me that when she and Graciana were younger you worked long hours but you always made time to help them with their homework so that they gained the required grades for them to go to university.'

'I wanted them to have the chance of good careers. Growing up in the *favela* where there was poor schooling made me realise that education is the means of escaping poverty. That is why, with Diego, I have established the Future Bright Foundation, which provides college funds for young people from the slums.'

The scent of lemons perfumed the night air. Sabrina took a soft breath, afraid to disturb the sense of companionship she felt with Cruz as he told her things about his life that he had never spoken of before.

'Tell me more about your career,' he invited. 'What made you decide to become a historian?'

She smiled. 'I grew up literally surrounded by history. Parts of Eversleigh Hall date back to the fifteen hundreds. I was always fascinated by the Bancroft family's connection to the estate, and history seemed a natural subject for me to study. I specialised in furniture restoration partly because the house has a large collection of antiques that needed to be restored.'

'Do you have any other ambitions, or do you plan to devote your life to Eversleigh?'

The question forced Sabrina to acknowledge that she had given so much of her time to the stately home and she had not considered what she wanted to do in the future, either in her career or her personal life. She might as well face it, she did not have a personal life, she thought dismally. She was twenty-eight, and if she did not take control of her destiny there was a good chance that another ten years would slip past without her achieving any of her dreams.

'I enjoy lecturing and I'd like to do more work at the university.' She hesitated. 'I would also like to have a family,' she admitted. 'Many of my friends are settling down and having children.'

Cruz shot her an intent look. 'I'm surprised that you want children. Ten years ago you did not seem happy when you became pregnant.'

They walked into the villa and Sabrina halted in the entrance hall and turned to face him.

'I *was* happy when I found out I was expecting a baby, but I also felt scared and alone. I was eighteen,' she reminded him, 'living in another country away from the familiar things I was used to in England, and I admit that I missed Eversleigh Hall and especially my brother. But when I tried to explain how I felt you didn't seem to care or understand, and you don't understand me any better now,' she said flatly.

She swung away from him, but Cruz caught hold of her arm. 'Then let me try to understand you. It's true that we didn't communicate enough back then. I had no idea that you felt scared of being pregnant because you never told me, and I now realise that my failure to talk about my mother's problems during her pregnancies caused misunderstandings between us.'

He pulled her into his arms and stared into her stormy grey eyes. 'We came to Quinta na Floresta so that we could discuss what happened in Brazil years ago. But I am more interested in looking forwards. Neither of us are the people we were then. We have developed, changed…' he gave a wry smile '…grown up. What if we stop thinking about the past, and instead spend our time here getting to know each other better, with no preconceptions?'

CHAPTER ELEVEN

SOMETHING STIRRED INSIDE SABRINA. It was too fragile to call it hope, but it was so infinitely precious that she was almost scared to breathe. 'Is that really what you want, a chance for us to learn more about the people we are now?'

'Yes.' His warm breath feathered her lips as he slanted his mouth over hers and kissed her with fierce passion and an unexpected tenderness that tugged on her heart.

'I'd like that, too,' she said huskily. Her smile stole Cruz's breath and he silently acknowledged that he had longed for her to smile at him unguardedly and without the shadow of mistrust in her eyes.

'We will make time to talk,' he promised. 'But when we make love we understand each other perfectly.' He lifted her into his arms and carried her up the stairs. 'Let me prove how well I understand your desires, *querida*.'

In the master bedroom slivers of pearl-grey moonlight slanted through the blinds and cast stripes across the bed and on Sabrina's body as Cruz undressed her. His hands smoothed over her skin as he slid her dress down her hips, awakening every tiny nerve-ending on her body to urgent life.

She would not have unrealistic expectations that Cruz's suggestion for them to get to know one another properly would lead to him wanting a meaningful relationship, she told herself firmly. But her thoughts scattered when he removed her bra and cupped her breasts in his hands, rubbing his thumb pads over her nipples until they hardened and reddened in anticipation of him taking each peak into his mouth.

He gave her a quick smile and she sensed that he was holding back. His words confirmed the idea. 'I want to caress every inch of your body, kiss every centimetre of your skin and discover every pleasure point as if this is our first time making love with each other,' he told her raggedly. 'I want to make it perfect for you.'

She cradled his face in her hands, loving the rough stubble on his jaw scraping her soft palms. 'You always make love to me perfectly.'

He would not be rushed, however much she pleaded and implored in a voice breathless with desire. His touch was as soft as gossamer as he stroked the undersides of her breasts before moving lower to slip between her thighs where he discovered that her knickers were damp with the slickness of her arousal.

'You are so beautiful,' he murmured as he eased the panel of her panties aside and ran a finger up and down her moist opening until she parted for him like the petals of a flower and he probed her, delicately at first and then more intensely, swirling one digit and then two inside her.

'Cruz…' She clutched his shoulders to steady herself, feeling her legs tremble, and murmured her approval when he bared her and laid her on the bed. She began to unbutton his shirt but he straightened up and swiftly removed his clothes himself.

She pouted. 'I wanted to undress you.'

'Not this time, *querida*. This is all about me giving you pleasure.' The sensual promise in his voice sent a quiver of excitement through her and she gave a voluptuous sigh when he knelt over her and kissed her mouth in a deeply erotic kiss. He moved down to her breasts and teased each nipple in turn with his tongue before he trailed a line of kisses to the apex between her legs and bestowed a shockingly intimate caress that made her lift her hips towards the powerful ridge of his erection.

She ran her hands over his chest and traced the ridges of his abdominal muscles, ignoring his protest as she moved lower and curled her fingers around his arousal. A shudder ran through him as she began to move her hand up and down, faster and faster until he groaned and rolled away from her to quickly sheath himself.

He entered her slowly, carefully, taking his time to allow her to absorb his length, and at the same time he claimed her mouth in a kiss that simmered with sensuality yet was so evocative that Sabrina thought she would die from the pleasure of it. When he began to move she met each deep thrust with such unguarded delight that Cruz's intention to make the loving long and slow was lost in the maelstrom of fierce passion that had always blazed between them.

With each steady stroke he took them both higher, increasing their mutual pleasure until the world no longer existed and there was just their own world of exquisite sensations building, building to a crescendo. Sabrina locked her ankles behind his back and drew him deeper inside her, taking each powerful thrust and wanting more, wanting it to never end and yet desperate, so desperate for the explosive climax that she knew was just ahead of her.

He caught her as she fell, and they tumbled into the abyss together wrapped in each other's arms, hearts pounding; two bodies in total accord, two souls connected. It was a long time before their breathing slowed and Cruz rolled off her, but he gave her no chance to slide across the bed and firmly drew her against him so that her head rested on his shoulder.

She smiled sleepily and kissed his satiny skin. There were things she wanted to say, things she was afraid to say, she acknowledged ruefully. Cruz had stated that he wanted to look forwards rather than dwell on the past, but Sabrina sensed that the shadow of the accident at the diamond mine and the fact that her father might have been responsible for Vitor Delgado's death still hung over them.

'What would you like to do today?'

Sabrina looked across the breakfast table at Cruz and her heart gave a familiar flip. Dressed in faded jeans and a tight-fitting white tee shirt, his black hair falling across his brow, he was as handsome as ever. But this was a different, more relaxed Cruz. He was a charming and entertaining companion and she loved spending leisurely days with him, relaxing by the pool at his villa or exploring the local area when they visited the beach or walked in the national park.

During the past two weeks that they had been

at Quinta na Floresta they had talked more than they had ever done ten years ago. It was different now, she mused. They were older, and she knew it was important to Cruz that they were financially equal, although she had never cared that when she had first met him in Brazil he had been a poor miner.

'The beach, I think,' she decided. 'And maybe we could visit that little market where they sell the hand-painted pottery.'

He looked amused. 'At this rate we're going to have trouble taking your collection of crockery on the plane when we fly back to England.'

'I suppose we will have to go back soon.' Some of the pleasure went out of the day. 'Diego will be impatient for you to carry on searching Eversleigh Hall for the map, and I have work commitments.' The thought of leaving Portugal seemed unbearable, especially as the future was uncertain. They talked about every subject under the sun, the glaring exception being their relationship. 'The last two weeks have been fun.'

'For me too,' he assured her. An indefinable

expression darkened his eyes. 'We can spend a few more days here in our private world,' he said softly. 'After we've visited the market, we'll have lunch at our favourite seafood restaurant before coming back here for a siesta.'

Sabrina threw him an impish smile. 'I thought a siesta is meant to be when you take a nap during the hottest part of the day.'

Cruz's sexy grin sent a tingle down to her toes. 'Well, you will be lying down, *querida*, but I can't promise that you will be sleeping.'

They spent the morning at a secluded beach that was only accessible by climbing down a steep, rocky path, which might have explained why they had the place to themselves.

'This is heavenly,' Sabrina murmured as she lay on a beach mat, enjoying the deliciously lazy feeling of the sun warming her skin. She opened her eyes as a shadow loomed over her, and gave Cruz an unguarded smile that stole his breath.

Growing up in the *favela*, he had never believed in a heaven, although he'd been well aware that there was a hell. But today was a perfect day, in a perfect place, and most perfect of all was Sabrina. He bent his head and kissed her, and her ardent response stirred his hunger. 'I need to go for a swim,' he said as he reluctantly lifted his mouth from hers.

'Are you too hot?' she asked innocently. Her gaze dropped to the bulge in his swim-shorts. 'Oh, I see that you're very hot.'

'Tease all you like, *querida*,' he growled. His eyes gleamed wickedly. 'But expect to be punished later.'

After lunch they strolled through the market and Sabrina stopped at a stall that sold exceptionally good watercolour paintings. 'The picture of the horse looks like Monty.' She gave a wistful sigh as she studied the painting of a chestnut-coloured horse with a dark brown mane.

'Thank you,' she murmured when Cruz paid for the picture and gave it to her. She glanced around at the other market stalls. 'Is there anything here that you want?'

He ran his eyes over her skimpy denim shorts and long, tanned legs and he felt his body stir.

'There is only one thing I want, *gatinha*. It's time we went home for that siesta.'

Cruz had parked his car in a side street behind the market. As he and Sabrina walked towards the silver Lamborghini, a football flew through the air and thudded onto the car's gleaming bonnet. A group of young boys tore up the street to reclaim the ball, but they stopped dead when they saw Cruz inspecting his beloved sports car for a scratch.

'Sinto muito!' One of the boys stepped forwards. He was skinny, with a mass of black hair and big dark eyes. His gaze darted to Sabrina's blonde hair and back to Cruz, and he must have assumed that they were tourists. 'Sorry!' he repeated in English. He stared at the Lamborghini and gave an irrepressible grin. 'Nice car, meester!'

Sabrina expected Cruz to react angrily. His car was his pride and joy, but he laughed and kicked the football towards the boy. 'Are you any good at football? I bet I can score a goal before you can.'

The gang of boys chased after Cruz down

the street while Sabrina leaned against a tree and watched the impromptu football match. He would have been a great father if their child had lived, she mused. Her heart ached as she imagined Cruz playing football with their son, who would have been a similar age to the boys.

He returned to the car ten minutes later, followed by the gang of boys, who looked suitably impressed when he started the powerful engine.

'I was a football-mad kid like those boys,' he told Sabrina as he drove back to the villa. His fingers tightened on the steering wheel. 'Sometimes I wonder what our son would have been like. If he'd have liked to play football, and shared my love of sports cars.' He gave her a wry smile. 'Maybe he would have been fascinated by history.'

She heard the sadness in his voice and her own sadness was mixed with a sense of guilt that had always haunted her, the belief that the miscarriage had been her fault.

By the time they arrived at Quinta na Floresta Sabrina's head throbbed with tension. Cruz looked at her closely, wondering why she suddenly seemed so remote after they had spent an enjoyable day together. Since they had come to Portugal he had discovered that the real Sabrina was very different from his previous opinion of her. Although she had grown up in a luxurious stately home, she had simple tastes, rather than wanting a champagne lifestyle as he had supposed. He had known she was intelligent, and she had revealed a dry sense of humour that he appreciated. She was the only woman who he had found that he genuinely enjoyed spending time with out of the bedroom.

He wished he could persuade her to tell him what was troubling her. 'Do you want to swim in the pool?'

'If you don't mind, I'd like to lie down for a while. I've got a pounding headache,' she admitted.

'You've probably had too much sun. Go to bed,' he said gently.

'I'm sure I'll feel fine after a nap.' Sabrina hurried up to their bedroom, needing to be alone with her thoughts. In her mind she heard the regret in Cruz's voice when he had spoken of their lost son and she felt as if a knot inside her were pulling so tight that it might snap.

She must have fallen straight to sleep because when she opened her eyes the room was rose-tinted with rays of sunset filtering through the slats. The clock showed that it was eight p.m. and she wondered if Cruz was waiting for her to go down to dinner. The idea of food made her stomach churn, but she told herself she would feel better after she'd splashed cold water on her face and caught her hair up into a loose knot.

The house was silent as she walked downstairs. Her feet instinctively took her outside to the courtyard where the soft splash of the fountain stirred the still air. The sun was a scarlet ball sinking in the sky and golden light lingered on the inscribed words around the fountain's base. Luiz, Luiz…the name formed a never-ending circle with no beginning and no end, just as there would be no end to her love for her little boy.

Her baby would always live in her heart.

The knot inside Sabrina broke and released a torrent of pain that she had held inside her for what seemed like a lifetime. She cried for the child she had lost and her excited hopes of motherhood that had been cruelly destroyed. Most of all she cried for all the empty years of loneliness without Cruz that she had endured and all the years ahead that stretched endlessly before her.

The pain kept coming in great waves that engulfed her and she sank down onto the wall of the fountain and buried her face in her hands as her shoulders shook with sobs.

Cruz found her there. He had been drawn to the courtyard when he'd heard a curious noise as a wounded animal might make; a sound of pain so raw that the sound of it had felt as if an arrow had pierced his heart.

Santa mãe! For a few seconds he could not comprehend what his eyes were seeing. Sabrina was sitting by the fountain, hunched over so that her head was almost resting on her knees, and the terrible, heart-rending cries were coming from her.

'Sabrina, are you ill? Tell me, are you in pain?' He put his hands on her shoulders and gently urged her to lift her head. The sight of her tear-streaked face shocked him. He had never seen her cry before and he recalled her telling him that her father had disapproved of displays of emotion.

She lifted her hands to her face to try and hide the evidence of her raw emotions, but Cruz wrapped his arms around her and held her tightly while her body shook with the storm of weeping.

'What is wrong, *querida*?' His voice roughened as he wondered if she was seriously ill.

Sabrina took a shuddering breath. 'You thought I didn't care about the miscarriage because I didn't show any emotion. But I did care, I wanted our baby. When I lost him, I felt numb inside but I couldn't cry because…' Her voice trembled and she could not go on.

'Because you had learned as a child not to show your emotions,' Cruz finished for her. 'You always had to be strong for your brother and you felt you must never let anyone see you crying.'

'I rushed back to Eversleigh so that I could

cry in private. I didn't stop to consider that you must be grieving for our child.' She wiped away her tears but they were immediately replaced by more. 'I know that you blamed me for the miscarriage.'

'Of course I didn't blame you,' he said gently. 'My mother's tragic losses had shown me that pregnancies don't always go to term.'

'I shouldn't have ridden my horse.'

He captured her chin and tilted her face up so that he could look into her eyes. 'My PA ran a half-marathon when she was four months pregnant and went on to have a healthy baby who arrived a week late. A reasonable amount of physical exercise is said to be good for expectant mothers. You were *not* responsible for losing our baby.'

Sabrina felt some of her tension lessen as she absorbed Cruz's words and realised that he truly did not think that she had jeopardised her pregnancy.

'You believed I rushed back to Eversleigh because I had decided that you were not good enough for me, but it wasn't true. I never cared that you didn't have much money,' she told him fiercely. 'When we met you were kind and interesting and you made me laugh a lot, and those are the important things. I admired you for being hard-working and risking your safety in the mine to earn money to support us. I left because I thought you blamed me for losing our child, and I couldn't bear it because I…' Her voice faltered as she realised that she was giving away too much of herself.

'Because you what, *querida*? Why did you leave?'

If they were going to stand any chance of having a relationship in the future they had to resolve the misunderstandings from the past. She took a swift breath. 'I was in love with you,' she said quietly.

Cruz's sculpted features showed no reaction, and after a moment Sabrina continued. 'You didn't understand why I refused to marry you. But I had seen my parents' marriage disintegrate into bitterness and resentment and I was afraid of that happening to us. I didn't want you to feel trapped in marriage because I had conceived your baby. After the miscarriage I thought you no longer wanted me, but leaving you was the hardest thing I have ever done and it broke my heart to say goodbye.'

She sighed. 'I wish we could turn the clock back. I wish we had been more open with each other ten years ago, but now it's too late.'

Cruz felt a pain in his chest as though his heart were being crushed by an iron fist. *Now it's too late!* He swallowed convulsively. *Deus*, it was the most heartbreaking statement he had ever heard because he knew it was true. Sabrina had said that she had loved him ten years ago. He noted she had used the past tense. But what else could he expect? He could not hope that Sabrina still loved him. Not after the appalling way he had treated her.

He stared at her tear-stained face and the pain inside him intensified as he acknowledged how he had misjudged her in the past, and since they had met again. When she had left Brazil he had thought she had rejected him because of the difference in their social status. But he now believed she genuinely had not cared that he'd earned low wages working in the diamond mine. She had admired him and she had loved him, but he had allowed his damnable pride to come between them.

The bitter irony was that he realised he had deserved her when he'd been poor. But now that he was wealthy, and financially they were equal, he absolutely did not deserve her. Sabrina's beauty was more than skin deep. She was a beautiful person, compassionate, caring and loyal to her family. It was for her brother's sake more than any other reason that she had desperately wanted to save Eversleigh Hall.

And what had he done? Cruz asked himself with savage self-contempt. He had offered her the money she needed to maintain the stately home, but in return he had demanded that she must become his mistress in a despicable deal that shamed him utterly and made a mockery of the fact that Sabrina had once admired him. There was nothing admirable about the way he had treated her and he knew that even if he spent the rest of his life apologising to her he could never deserve her now.

CHAPTER TWELVE

SABRINA FELT DRAINED after her emotional breakdown. She got unsteadily to her feet and would have stumbled but Cruz caught her and lifted her into his arms, carrying her into the house and up the stairs to their bedroom as if she weighed nothing. Neither of them spoke but she sensed that he had been shocked by her revelation that she had loved him ten years ago.

When he had demanded that she became his mistress he had made it clear that he only wanted her for sex, she remembered. But while they had been in Portugal they had, at his suggestion, spent time getting to know each other and she had felt hopeful that their affair might develop into a meaningful relationship. His unfathomable expression gave her the sinking feeling that she had blown it.

He set her down on the end of the bed and

headed into the en-suite bathroom, and moments later Sabrina heard the bath filling. She was so tired she could have fallen asleep in her clothes, but she allowed Cruz to undress her and help her into a foaming bath that smelled divinely of jasmine-scented bubbles. He took care of her as if she were a child, sponging her body and washing and rinsing her hair with such gentleness that more tears filled her eyes.

When the water started to cool he wrapped her in a fluffy towel and dried her. He slipped a silky nightgown over her head before he led her out onto the balcony where one of the household staff was finishing placing dishes of food on the table.

'You need to eat,' Cruz insisted when they were alone again. Sabrina doubted she could swallow food, but he had gone to such effort, and to please him she forced herself to eat some of the herb omelette he served her. To her surprise she felt better after she'd eaten a few mouthfuls. The experience of being cared for was new to her and she was reluctant to say anything that might shatter the fragile bond she felt with him.

After they had finished the meal he led her back into the bedroom and pulled back the covers for her to slide into bed. The sheets felt deliciously cool against her skin, and as she watched him strip off his jeans, tee shirt and boxer shorts she felt a familiar throb of desire low in her pelvis.

Cruz lay down beside her and drew her into his arms, but to her disappointment he turned her onto her side. 'You need to sleep,' he told her in a curiously taut voice. 'We'll talk in the morning.'

For a reason she could not define the promise filled her with unease and she stayed awake long after she heard his breathing settle into a steady rhythm.

She was unaware that Cruz's will power was tested to its limits as he remained awake and forced himself to resist the temptation to make love to Sabrina. He bitterly regretted that he had coerced her into being his mistress, and the price of his shameful behaviour was the knowledge that she would never be his.

Sabrina was woken by a persistent noise that as the fog of sleep cleared from her brain she recognised was her phone. The clock revealed that it was nearly ten a.m. and she discovered that she was alone in the bed. Tristan's name flashed on the phone's screen and she quickly answered the call.

'Tris—is everything okay?'

'Good news. Dad's come home,' Tristan announced. 'He turned up at the British Embassy in Guinea a week ago without money or belongings and told them he had been seriously ill after contracting a tropical disease. He had been staying in a remote village and as a result of a high fever he had lost his memory for months. He arrived at Eversleigh yesterday and he's impatient to see you. Apparently he has an idea for making money for the estate and he wants to put you in charge.'

It was typical of her father to make plans that involved her without pausing to consider that she had her own life, Sabrina thought ruefully.

But she was relieved that he was safe and well. She was used to the earl's eccentricities and although he had not been the best father when she had been growing up, she was fond of him.

Cruz was outside on the balcony. He appeared to be deep in his thoughts and although he smiled when he saw her, Sabrina noted that his smile did not reach his eyes. She relayed Tristan's message. 'I'd like to go home to see Dad,' she said. 'We were due to go back to Eversleigh in a few days anyway.'

Cruz did not immediately reply and his shuttered expression gave no clue to his thoughts. Sabrina felt a strange sense of unease as she had done the previous night when he had said that they would talk in the morning. Something about him had changed. Was it coincidence that he seemed tense this morning after she had confessed that she had loved him in Brazil? His words confirmed her fears.

'It will be better if you go back to Eversleigh and see your father on your own.'

'I thought you would want to ask him about the map.'

'I no longer care about finding the map.'

She stared at him. 'But the map was the reason you moved into Eversleigh Hall.'

'That's what I told myself,' he said in an odd voice that sounded as if he was mocking himself. 'I have decided to give my share of the Montes Claros mine to Diego. He will have geological surveys carried out to find out if there are old, deeper mineshafts, and if he finds more diamonds I wish him well. But the mine holds too many bad memories and I want to sever my connections to the past.'

He sounded so grim, and so final. Sabrina bit her lip. Was she part of the past that Cruz wanted to leave behind?

'If you don't want me to go to Eversleigh I'll stay here…or go with you to wherever your next business meeting is as I agreed when we made our deal,' she offered tentatively.

'Ah, yes, our deal!' He looked at her broodingly and she was startled by the flicker of pain she thought she glimpsed in his eyes before his expression hardened. He swung round and looked out over the balcony at the gardens.

Sabrina had the idea that he would rather look anywhere than at her.

'It's over,' he said tersely. 'I am releasing you from our arrangement and you no longer have to be my mistress.'

Shock stole her breath so that she could not speak. But even if she could, she did not know what to say. Pride prevented her from asking him *why*, and she would not plead with him to allow her to stay. It was clear to her that by revealing that she had loved him ten years ago she had overstepped a boundary. He had not wanted her love then and he did not want it now.

Her throat ached with tears, but she swallowed hard, determined not to break down in front of him. She dug deep into her reservoir of mental strength and managed to answer him with cool composure. 'In that case I had better go and pack.'

Cruz did not turn round but he sensed that Sabrina had walked into the bedroom and minutes later he heard the sound of a suitcase zip. He clenched his hands on the balcony rail until his knuckles felt as if they would split open.

This was what he had to do, he reminded himself. He had to let her go because she deserved to meet someone far better than him. He was so bitterly ashamed of how he had treated her that he could not even bring himself to look at her because surely he would see disgust in her eyes where once there had been love, if only he had not been too blind to see it.

It had been raining ever since Sabrina had arrived back at Eversleigh Hall three days ago. The depressing weather echoed her mood as she stared out of the window and watched the geraniums being battered to death.

'You don't look very happy,' Earl Bancroft commented. 'What's the matter with you?'

'Nothing.' She blinked away her tears before she turned to face her father.

'Tristan told me you were dating Cruz Delgado again. Do you think that was wise after he broke your heart years ago?'

'Probably not,' she said dully. 'Anyway, I won't be seeing him again.' Ever. The knowledge felt as if a knife had been plunged through her heart. She forced herself to concentrate on her father, who looked in remarkably good health. 'I'm glad you are okay. I was worried about you.'

'Were you?' he said casually. 'You should have known I'd turn up sooner or later.'

'Tris mentioned that you have plans for Eversleigh Hall.'

'Ah, yes. I've had the brilliant idea of turning the estate into a wild animal park.' The earl ignored Sabrina's startled expression. 'You know the sort of thing, lions and tigers in enclosures, and monkeys. I thought of basing myself in Africa so that I could arrange for animals to be shipped over to England.'

'So, who will organise the animal park here at Eversleigh?'

'You will, of course.'

She stared at her father, feeling exasperated by his assumption that she would remain at Eversleigh for ever, like a lonely Victorian spinster, she thought bleakly. 'Have you ever thought that I might have other plans for my life?'

Earl Bancroft looked intently at his daughter. 'I have a feeling that you would like your plans for the future to include Delgado.'

Sabrina did not deny it. 'When I left Brazil and came back to Eversleigh ten years ago, why didn't you tell me that there had been an accident at the mine and Cruz's father had been killed?'

Her father sighed. 'I felt guilty that I hadn't tried harder to convince Vitor not to go into the deepest section of the mine. I knew the roof supports were unstable and I had arranged for them to be reinforced, but the work was delayed.'

'Did you send Vitor back to look for more diamonds that might have been as valuable as the Red Star?'

'Good heavens, no! I pleaded with him not to go back, but he was obsessed with finding a diamond that would make him rich. They call it diamond fever, and Vitor had it badly. After his death, I decided to sell the mine. When I came back to Eversleigh that summer I didn't tell you about the accident because I knew you were suffering after you had lost a baby. You were so thin and pale, drifting around the house like a ghost. I was relieved when you decided to go to university that autumn and it seemed best not to mention what had happened in Brazil.'

The earl gave her a speculative look. 'Cruz is a decent man, from what I've heard. He and his business partner, Cazorra, have pushed for improvements to safety in Brazil's mining industry, and they pour money into a charity they set up to help children living in the *favelas.* I guessed that you fell in love with him ten years ago. Is there a chance that the two of you will get back together?'

Sabrina turned her head towards the window so that her father would not see her tears as she remembered Cruz's unyielding expression when he had sent her away from Quinta na Floresta. 'No, there is no chance,' she whispered.

'Why didn't you tell me the truth about Papai's accident before now?' Cruz spoke in Portuguese. He leapt up from the sofa in his mother's house and dragged oxygen into his lungs as he tried to come to terms with her shocking revelation. 'Why did you allow me to think for all these years that Earl Bancroft had forced Vitor to go back into an unsafe area of the mine?'

'I was afraid that if I told you what had really happened, you would think less of your father.' Ana-Maria wiped tears from her face. 'Vitor was a good man but he became obsessed with finding another valuable diamond like the Estrela Vermelha. His obsession became almost like an illness. He would not listen to me or to Earl Bancroft, who pleaded with Vitor not to go into the deepest part of the mine until the roof supports had been strengthened. Your father ignored the earl's advice and lost his life as a result.'

'Deus.' Cruz dropped his head into his hands. 'I wish I had known.'

'You blamed the earl and believed that Vitor was a hero, and I saw no reason to tell you the truth,' his mother admitted. 'You had idolised your father when he was alive, and I wanted you to carry on feeling proud of his memory. I realised I should tell you how the accident had really happened when you brought the Bancroft girl here and I saw your face when you looked at her. But I did not say anything these past weeks because Sabrina broke your heart once and I was worried she might do so again.' She hurried after Cruz as he strode towards the front door. 'What will you do now?'

His jaw clenched. 'Obviously I need to apologise to Sabrina for my unfair accusation that her father was responsible for Vitor's death.'

Deus, he had so much to apologise to Sabrina for, Cruz thought grimly. He kissed his mother's cheek and walked out of her house, craving solitude while he tried to come to terms with what she had told him. It was true he had idolised his father, and with hindsight he realised that he had *wanted* to blame Earl Bancroft for Vitor's accident rather than accept that Vitor's obsession with diamonds had ultimately resulted in his death.

He had allowed his skewered view of events that had happened ten years ago to affect his opinion of Sabrina, Cruz acknowledged grimly. When he'd taken the time to get to know her properly, he had discovered that she was as lovely as the girl he had fallen for years ago. He'd sent her away because he was consumed with guilt at the way he had treated her and he believed he did not deserve her.

But she had loved him once.

Perhaps she could fall in love with him again?

His heart was hammering and his steps slowed as another thought rocked him to his core. Was he allowing his guilt at how he had behaved with Sabrina to stop him from fighting for her? He had told himself he was doing the honourable thing by letting her go. But he was a coward, Cruz told himself contemptuously. All his life he had fought for the things that mattered to him. He had escaped poverty and fought to take care of his family. So why the hell wasn't he fighting for the person who he now realised mattered to him more than anything in the world? Yes, he was ashamed of how he had treated Sabrina, and if she rejected him it would be nothing more than he deserved. But he could not, *would* not, allow his guilty conscience to hold him back from going after her.

* * *

Sabrina was thankful that her father quickly lost interest in his idea of creating a wild animal park but her relief was short-lived when he announced that he was thinking of starting an alpaca farm. The truth was she did not care what happened to Eversleigh Hall, which, a few months ago, would have been unthinkable. For the past ten years she had devoted all her time and energy to her family's stately home, but she had poured her emotions into Eversleigh to hide from the fact that she had never stopped loving Cruz.

Unable to concentrate on her latest furniture-restoration project, she walked listlessly around the estate. The hawthorn bushes along the lane were covered with tiny white flowers that smelled divine, but the beauty of the Surrey countryside in early summer failed to lift her from her black hole of misery. Out of habit her feet took her in the direction of the stables. She was even imagining that she was hearing things, she thought despairingly. But her heart gave a jolt when she recognised a familiar whinnying from the other side of the beech hedge.

As she walked across the yard she told herself she must actually have lost her sanity, and her eyes were deceiving her. But there was no mistaking the chestnut-coloured head that appeared over the stable door. Monty greeted her with the snuffling sound she had missed so much, and when she lifted a trembling hand to pat him, he nuzzled his face into her neck.

Nothing made sense. How could her beloved horse be back at Eversleigh? Something at the back of the stable caught her attention and she discovered it was a package addressed to her. She opened it with trembling fingers and stared at the painting of a horse that Cruz had bought for her from the market in Portugal. She had forgotten to pack the picture when he had sent her away from Quinta na Floresta.

How had the picture got here…? Unless…

She jerked her head round and made an inarticulate sound when she saw Cruz standing in the yard. Her brain registered that he looked utterly gorgeous in black jeans and a polo shirt topped with a tan leather jacket. She closed her eyes, but when she opened them again he was still there, still real, still the keeper of her heart as he would always be.

Her voice shook. 'Why are you here?'

His smile held faint irony. 'I think I've proved that I can't keep away from you, Sabrina, *meu amor*.'

My love! She only knew a few words of Portuguese but she told herself she must have misunderstood him.

'I wanted to deliver Monty in person. I know how much you love him,' he said softly. 'I tracked down his new owners and persuaded them to sell him. Now he is yours for ever.'

She bit her lip. 'I don't understand. You told me you don't want me to be your mistress.'

'It's true, I don't.'

She stifled a gasp of pain. 'Then why did you go to the effort of finding my horse?' She dared not hope that his gesture of returning Monty to her meant anything. But as she stared at his face she saw deep grooves beside his mouth and an expression of wretched despair in his eyes that she knew was mirrored in hers.

'Cruz…' Her feet had been rooted to the ground but suddenly she was able to move and she ran to him, not caring that she was giving away the secret she had tried to keep hidden from him for the past weeks. She was tired of pretending that she felt nothing for him. Ten years ago she had been too unsure of herself to fight for the man she loved, but she was determined to fight for him now, even if it meant risking his rejection.

Tears streamed down her face as she flung her arms around his neck. 'I'm sorry I left you years ago.'

'*You're* sorry?' Cruz groaned. 'You have nothing to be sorry for. I'm the one who should apologise for wrongly accusing your father, and especially for the way I treated you.'

Sabrina eased away from him so that she could look at his face, but he pulled her hard against his chest and wrapped his arms around her, holding her so tightly that she felt the uneven thud of his heart.

'My mother told me the truth about my father's accident,' he explained. 'Your father did not send Vitor back to search for more diamonds. Papai chose to go back into the mine against Earl Bancroft's advice. His obsession with finding diamonds made him ignore the risks and it was because of his decision that he left behind a grieving widow and two little girls without a father, and left a son so full of anger and bitterness that I behaved in a way that shames me,' he said roughly. 'I came to Eversleigh Hall to demand the map of the diamond mine from your father, but instead I met you and from the moment I saw you I was determined to have you in my bed again.' His voice was laced with self-contempt. 'Hardly the most noble ambition, but at the time I believed I had a right to want revenge for my father's death and I was angry that you had left me ten years ago. Believe me, *querida*, when I say that I deeply regret forcing you to become my mistress.'

Sabrina shook her head. 'You didn't force me.'

'I used your love for your home to blackmail you into selling yourself to me.'

'I chose to be your mistress for one reason only,' she said fiercely. 'It wasn't to save Eversleigh or to help my brother.' She met his gaze fearlessly. 'It was because I wanted *you*, the only man I have ever desired…and the only man I have ever loved and will love for the rest of my life.'

'Sabrina,' Cruz said hoarsely. But she hadn't finished. She had found the courage to open her heart and now she could not hold back her emotions.

'I wish you hadn't made your fortune, because then I could prove to you that I love you for who you are, a wonderful man who took care of his family and worked hard to support them, a man who will never forget the hardship he endured as a child and has set up a charity to help other children living in poverty in the *favelas*. I would be proud to marry you if you were penniless because love is more precious than anything.'

She looked at him with her heart in her eyes.

'I wish I had been brave enough to accept your marriage proposal ten years ago. I wish I had stayed in Brazil with you.'

'I wish I hadn't let you leave. I should have told you that the reason I had asked you to marry me was because I loved you.' He gently stroked her hair back from her face. 'I won't make the same mistake a second time, *meu amor*.'

There was a catch in Cruz's voice as Sabrina's words swirled in his heart and healed the ache that had been with him for so long that he was almost scared to believe that her beautiful smile was for him and him alone.

'I love you so much it hurts,' he said rawly.

'Cruz…my love.' Sabrina could hardly speak through her tears, but there was no need for words as he claimed her mouth, kissing her with passion and a bone-shaking tenderness that revealed the true depths of his love for her.

'*Eu te adoro*, I adore you.' He whispered the words over and over again, in between taking soft sips from her lips, beguiling her with his tender adoration. She made a small sound of protest when he lifted his mouth from hers, but then caught her breath as he dropped down onto one knee in front of her and took a small square box from his jacket pocket.

The solitaire white diamond ring sparkled in the sunshine that had emerged from behind the clouds. The square-cut precious gem was flawless, perfect, just as Sabrina was perfect, Cruz thought. 'Will you marry me, *meu anjo*, my angel, and be my only love for the rest of our lives?'

'Willingly, and so very happily,' she said, blinking back more tears as he slid the ring onto her finger. 'But we won't love each other exclusively.' Her voice shook a little. 'We will always love our first baby, Luiz. And hopefully there will be more children for us to love. I'd like at least four,' she told him with a teasing smile that Cruz knew would hold his heart prisoner for ever.

'Only four?' He swung her up in his arms and strode into the hay barn, pausing to secure the latch on the door so that they would not be disturbed.

'I don't think we should wait to start trying for a family.' Sabrina pulled off her tee shirt and bra and felt a delicious shiver of anticipation run through her as she watched Cruz sling his jacket on top of a hay bale, followed by his shirt, and move his hand to the zip of his jeans.

'Indeed,' he murmured, 'and when do you think would be a good time to start trying, *gatinha*?'

'Right now.' She stepped out of her skirt and panties and smiled when he drew an audible breath.

'How do you feel about holding our wedding here at Eversleigh Hall, followed by a honeymoon in the Seychelles…' he paused for a heartbeat '…and making our home at Quinta na Floresta? There are stables for Monty, and your cat can move in too, if you insist.'

'Of course we must take George with us.' Sabrina linked her arms around Cruz's neck and felt his very hard arousal push between her thighs. Her eyes gleamed wickedly. 'I love him almost as much as I love you.'

'I'm glad you said almost—' Cruz pushed

her flat on her back on a hay bale and grinned at her gasp of surprise as he surged into her '—because I plan on being the number one male in your life for ever, *meu amor*.'

'For ever sounds perfect,' she agreed.

* * * * *

If you enjoyed this story don't miss
Chantelle Shaw's conclusion
to her fabulous duet
BOUGHT BY THE BRAZILIAN *in...*
MASTER OF HER INNOCENCE
Coming soon!

MILLS & BOON®

Large Print – May 2016

The Queen's New Year Secret
Maisey Yates

Wearing the De Angelis Ring
Cathy Williams

The Cost of the Forbidden
Carol Marinelli

Mistress of His Revenge
Chantelle Shaw

Theseus Discovers His Heir
Michelle Smart

The Marriage He Must Keep
Dani Collins

Awakening the Ravensdale Heiress
Melanie Milburne

His Princess of Convenience
Rebecca Winters

Holiday with the Millionaire
Scarlet Wilson

The Husband She'd Never Met
Barbara Hannay

Unlocking Her Boss's Heart
Christy McKellen

MILLS & BOON®

Large Print – June 2016

Leonetti's Housekeeper Bride
Lynne Graham

The Surprise De Angelis Baby
Cathy Williams

Castelli's Virgin Widow
Caitlin Crews

The Consequence He Must Claim
Dani Collins

Helios Crowns His Mistress
Michelle Smart

Illicit Night with the Greek
Susanna Carr

The Sheikh's Pregnant Prisoner
Tara Pammi

Saved by the CEO
Barbara Wallace

Pregnant with a Royal Baby!
Susan Meier

A Deal to Mend Their Marriage
Michelle Douglas

Swept into the Rich Man's World
Katrina Cudmore